Santa Maybe

Santa Maybe

AUBREY MACE

CFI
Springville, Utah

ISBN 13: 978-1-59955-312-2

Published by CFI, an imprint of Cedar Fort, Inc., 2373 W. 700 S., Springville, UT 84663
Distributed by Cedar Fort, Inc., www.cedarfort.com

LIBRARY OF CONGRESS CATALOGING-IN-PUBLICATION DATA

Mace, Aubrey.
 Santa Maybe / Aubrey Mace.
  p. cm.
 ISBN 978-1-59955-312-2 (acid-free paper)
 1. Single women—Fiction. 2. Mate selection—Fiction. 3. Santa Claus—Fiction. I. Title.

 PS3613.A2717S26 2009
 813'.6--dc22
                    2009009361

Cover design by Jen Boss
Cover design © 2009 by Lyle Mortimer
Edited and typeset by Heidi Doxey

Printed in the United States of America

10 9 8 7 6 5 4 3 2 1

Printed on acid-free paper

Dedication

For my dads . . . both of them.

To Ron, who keeps telling me how famous I'm going to be. If it ever happens, I promise to drag you along with me.

And to Glenn, who taught me about oatmeal raisin cookies, among other things.

I love you both so much.

And last but not least, to my brother-in-law David, the original Mr. Fanta, no ice.

Acknowledgments

Writing is such a solitary affair. One of the biggest rewards for me is when a person takes the time not only to read something I wrote, but goes one step further and tracks me down to tell me they liked it. It's still such a huge deal for me when someone says they read one of my books. It's a surreal, thrilling experience, and I don't think it will ever lose its magic. So, thanks to all of you—you can't imagine how your words have brightened my days.

Much thanks to all my friends at Cedar Fort, old and new. You have made this wild ride a little smoother for me, and I feel privileged to know everyone I have met there.

And finally, thanks to my critique group girls, Sue Marchant and Melanie Jacobson. Sue, thanks for your support—I hope I get to see your book soon! Melanie, thanks for your valuable insights, writing chocolate, and your friendship. Oh . . . and the title. ☺

Other books by Aubrey Mace

Spare Change
My Fairy Grandmother

Prologue

* * * * * * * * * *

When I was younger, I fell in love like most people change their socks. My first love was in kindergarten. The boy who sat next to me passed me a little bag of peanuts under the desk, and that was it. We were soul mates. That is, until I caught him chasing Jamie Stevens around the playground, trying to trip her. Everyone knows that in grade school, when a boy torments you, he's obviously in love. I was heartbroken. But it didn't take long before I was in hot pursuit of my next conquest. I was what my dad referred to as boy crazy.

In my life, I, Abbie Canfield, have been in love no less than forty-seven times, probably more if you count the names that didn't make it onto The List. Yes, I used to keep a list, but I misplaced it somewhere toward the end of high school. Each time, I carefully scrawled the name of my beloved in pen—since we would be together for all time, there was obviously no need for erasers. I found The List in a box about a year ago and noted with amusement that some of the later entries were inscribed in pencil instead. At least I was learning.

What was the one thing this myriad of males had in common? They were all perfect for me. Birds sang in a cloudless, sunny sky, and I walked around with a smile on my face and a permanent soundtrack of love songs playing in my head. Until, for whatever reason, one by one, they moved on.

I planned, to some extent, six different weddings in various stages and degrees of completion. I chose five different styles of bridesmaid's dresses, four wedding cakes, put down a deposit on three reception centers, went through two complete bridal portrait sessions, and watched one ceremonial release of a flock of doves . . . by myself. (The fee was non-refundable, so I went through with it anyway. I wanted to get something for my money.) And when my relationships crumbled, I was devastated for as long as it took to meet my next Mr. Wonderful. I was, for lack of a better term, a hopeless romantic.

Until one day, I lost hope.

As I watched those doves soar off into the deep, blue sky, I thought, *This is supposed to be the happiest day of my life.* The dove lady gave me a sympathetic pat on the arm before she got in her car and sped off, leaving me to my thoughts. Even though I'd had my doubts over the years, I'd always managed to bury them under a layer of optimism. Unfortunately, there isn't enough optimism in the world to gloss over *that* many botched attempts at love. I couldn't argue anymore with the little voice in my head. I was in my early thirties, having just been dumped by yet another potential husband, and suddenly, it was painfully clear.

This just wasn't meant to happen for me.

Ever since then, I've been resigned to my plight. I've accepted my single status.

I've surrendered . . . to spinsterhood.

When I stopped looking at every man I passed on the street, wondering if he could be the love of my life, an interesting thing happened.

Well, actually, nothing happened. But instead of being disappointed and sad that I hadn't met someone, I didn't even think about it anymore. Since I no longer expected love around every corner, I had no reason to be blue when I didn't find it.

Which wasn't to say I was never lonely. There were those pathetic days now and then when I ended up in my bed watching weepy romance movies and picturing myself in the lead role, or at Barnes and Noble, wearing a pair of dark glasses to hide my puffy eyes, perusing through a big stack of bridal magazines and armed with an even bigger stack of Kleenex.

I wish I was kidding.

But for the most part, things were okay for me. I decided that there are much worse things in life than being single. I used all the free time that was previously devoted to man hunting to do some of the things I'd always wanted to. I love to cook and try new recipes, so I got a small business loan and opened my own bakery called Just Desserts. People said I was crazy and I would never make it, but somehow, I survived. I put all my energy into making it succeed and, against all odds, it did. My bakery has been open for five years now, and I can truly say that I have my dream job. I love going to work in the morning, and it makes me happy to see people's faces when they discover their favorite treat in the glass case.

So, my life was falling into place quite nicely. With the exception of romance, I had everything a girl could want. Little did I know that the universe was about to take everything I knew about relationships and turn it inside out. It all started right before Christmas . . .

One Year Earlier . . .

✳ ✳✳ ✵ ✳ ✳✳

One

It was the night of December 23, and I was trying to finish boxing up the Santa cookies before the rush tomorrow morning. Despite my best efforts, I had fallen behind on my orders and ended up staying late, not wanting anyone to be disappointed. My sister Grace even showed up for a while, abandoning her husband and children to help me. When I opened the door, she was standing there shivering, holding two Super Big Gulps. I'd never been so thrilled to see anyone in my life.

"I'm so glad you came. For a minute, I was afraid I wouldn't be able to fill all the orders, even if I stayed all night. I'm going to have to hire a few part-timers in December next year."

"Trust me, I was happy to come. The kids are driving me crazy, trying to figure out where I've hidden their presents."

I grinned. "You should have just told them they were at my house. Maybe they'd leave you alone."

"They don't give up that easily. They'd just think I was trying to throw them off the trail."

For some reason, the whole Cookies for Santa idea had really taken off this year. Since I first opened the bakery, I'd baked thick, soft sugar cookies iced in gooey white frosting and sprinkled them with red and green sugar crystals. I made them the week before Christmas so kids could leave them out for Santa Claus, and I had a few loyal customers. But it was nothing like the flood of orders I'd received this year.

The sudden increase in business might have been due to my brother-in-law Jack's brilliant promotional plan. Jack is in advertising, and what he lacked in common sense, he made up for in business. He drew up some eye-catching signs, announcing that my bakery carried Santa's Favorite Cookies, and he even had some boxes made for me. They were plain white, their only decoration a very official looking Santa's Stamp of Approval. I had to admit, I was impressed.

My sister was helping me add the final touch to the boxes, tying them up with colored twine. People had been pre-ordering cookies for months, and now that Christmas was finally here, they would be descending on my store to pick them up. From the sheer volume I was selling, I hoped that Santa wouldn't be eating all of them. Otherwise, he might have a little trouble getting back into the sleigh to return to the North Pole.

"Is all of your shopping finished?" I asked, licking a little bit of frosting off my wrist.

"Almost. There are only one or two things left I need to pick up after looking at the Christmas lists."

"Oh, I remember when we used to make our Christmas lists," I said wistfully. "We'd go through that big catalogue and circle all the things we wanted. And then, remember how we'd look through it a hundred times to make sure we hadn't missed anything important before we sat down to make our final lists?"

She nodded. "The kids did theirs online this year."

"Online?"

"Yeah, there's this website where you can go to email your list to Santa. You can even attach links to other websites, so Santa can see exactly which toy you're hoping for. Apparently, all the kids are doing it." She paused, a thoughtful expression on her face. "Why is it that my kids can attach documents to their emails, but I still can't figure it out?"

"I know. I guess the world has moved on. Internet lists just don't have the same feeling, do they?"

We continued working in silence for a minute, me carefully layering the cookies between layers of wax paper in the boxes and Grace securing them with the twine. Maybe it was the holiday season or maybe it was the lateness and the toll of my eighteen-hour day, but I was feeling a little down. Without realizing it, I let out an enormous sigh.

"You must be exhausted," Grace said.

I smiled while rotating my neck, trying to ease a stubborn kink. "Christmas is hard."

"I know. There's the shopping, and the cooking, and the cards, and the wrapping, and the entertaining—"

"That's not exactly what I meant. I was talking about being single. It's kind of lonely."

"Yes, I remember the last time I was lonely," she mused. "It was when I was in labor with my first, and my darling husband went to find the vending machine and didn't come back for an hour and a half. I don't think I've been alone once since then."

"I guess the grass is always greener. When I go into the store and see all the families shopping together and the kids waiting in line with their parents to see Santa, it makes me kind of sad."

My sister's face lit up suddenly. "You should do it!"

"I should do what?"

"You should go to the website and tell Santa that you want a husband for Christmas!"

I snorted. "Yeah, right."

"I'm serious! It's a great idea."

"Gracie, it's not like when we used to browse through the catalogue. You can't just check a box and wait for a man to arrive."

"It's definitely worth a try. Plus, I read somewhere that when you write a goal down, it makes it much more concrete."

"That's for someone who wants to get out of debt or lose

ten pounds, not someone who's hoping to find a spouse in her stocking."

"Well, I think you should do it. What harm could it do?"

I took one of the cookies off the tray and passed it to her. "Here, eat this. You're obviously so delirious with hunger that you're not making sense any more."

She broke the cookie in half and sunk her teeth into it happily. My sister is the mother of three children, eats pastries like they're going out of style, and manages to remain bone thin. I, on the other hand am careful about what I eat, torture myself on the treadmill four to five days a week, and watch the pounds climb on even if all I do is look at cookies. In retrospect, owning a bakery is probably not the job most suited to maintaining my ideal weight, but you know what they say; never trust a skinny cook. I try to think of myself as pleasantly rounded or . . . curvy. I suppose I'm about average where body size is concerned, but I have to work at it. And it's difficult not to be envious when Grace wolfs three brownies in a sitting and the scale doesn't budge.

As if able to read my thoughts, she mumbled, "I swear I could eat a dozen of these. How do you stay so skinny working here?"

"Please. I'm a horse."

She brushed her hands off on her apron before untying it. "No, you're not. You're perfect. Now, I'd better get home. I have a ton of wrapping left to do, and Jack probably let the kids destroy the house while I was gone. It's amazing how much damage they can do in just a few hours. Sometimes I'm tempted to set up a hidden camera, just to see how it happens."

I walked her to the door and hugged her. "Thank you so much for coming—you're a lifesaver. I'll bring your cookies by tomorrow night."

It was freezing cold outside, and I could see her breath as she shouted at me from her car. "You really should get online and send Santa your list. He can't bring you what you want if you don't ask."

I ignored the bait. "Drive safe, okay?"

"They say there's someone for everyone out there," she said in a singsong voice.

"Time to go home now," I sang back.

I closed the door behind her, locking it before going back into the kitchen. I filled the sink with hot, soapy water, watching as the remnants of sticky frosting melted away. The sink faced a window and as I washed the dishes, I could see flurries of fat snowflakes in the narrow swath of light from a streetlamp, quickly beginning to cover the ground.

When I finished it was after midnight, and I decided I'd better get home myself since I had to be back here in a few hours. I bundled up in my coat, scarf, earmuffs, gloves, and boots before going outside. Some children had built a snowman in front of the bakery days ago, but the weather had been so cold lately that he was still around. His eyes had disappeared, but the carrot I gave them for his nose was still attached, as was most of the raisin mouth. I gathered up some rocks, giving him new, makeshift eyes. Now that he could see the fresh snow falling around him, he looked quite cold and miserable. I wound my scarf around his neck and loaned him my earmuffs before jumping into my car to drive home.

Two

"Make sure and save some of those cookies for Santa, okay?" I said, waving to a mother and her two kids who'd stopped in to pick up their order. The bell on the door rang cheerily as it closed behind them. I crossed their names off my list of people who had pre-ordered, carefully figuring how many extra I had for people who just walked in. It looked like I would sell out for sure, but according to my calculations, there should be a few boxes left for people who'd waited until the last minute.

It had been a busy day so far, with plenty of kids eager to secure their cookies to sweeten up Santa, accompanied by plenty of parents who were eager to be one step closer to finishing their chores so that they could go home and collapse. To them, I was just one more item to cross off on their never-ending to-do list. Everyone was a little frazzled, but one woman seemed even more frazzled than most.

Her name was Bonnie, and she came into the bakery about once a week. She was always friendly, but in a distracted sort of way. She always came alone, and every bit of her was over processed; from her frizzy blonde hair to her seemingly fragile mental state. For instance, most people walk right up to the glass case, giving it a cursory glance before making their decision. But no matter how many times Bonnie came in, she always looked lost. She lingered near the back before wandering up to the counter slowly, as if she were in some sort of a fog. When she finally arrived, she seemed overwhelmed by the number of choices. She might have stood there forever if I didn't interrupt, asking if there was anything I could help her with. After I'd spoken to her, the spell was broken, and she was always very aware and present. I think it had something to do with the fact that, after I'd seen her a few times, she revealed she had seven kids under the age of ten. The very idea of maintaining order over that brood was enough to make anyone's eyes cloud over.

Today was a first—she brought all the kids in. They swarmed in circles around her, like little bees buzzing, bouncing crazily off the parental hive. I started to wonder if the reason she looked so shell-shocked every time I saw her was because her solo trip to the bakery was the only chance she ever got to let her mind wander. Her visit was only about ten minutes long, consisting of two minutes of small talk, one minute of paying for her cookies, and seven minutes of trying to gather her children to leave. No sooner had she rounded them up than one would escape, giving the others an opportunity to flee while she tried to retrieve the latest escapee. It appeared that the kids were trying to make their field trip last as long as possible. When she finally had them all organized, Bonnie paused briefly after pushing the last one out the door ahead of her.

"You don't have any kids, do you, Abbie?"

"No," I said, shrugging my shoulders.

I noticed the lines etched deep into the skin around her eyes. She looked like she'd aged ten years in the last ten minutes. "You don't know how lucky you are," she said, sighing deeply. The bell clanked as the door slammed behind her, but it sounded angry this time.

I got a wet rag from the kitchen, trudging out to the tables. I'd spied one of Bonnie's kids playing with the sugar, dumping it out of the container and watching, mystified, as it cascaded onto the table. I mopped up the mess, suddenly feeling very old and unwanted. I was sure Bonnie hadn't meant any harm by her comment, but it only served to remind me that I was childless and alone . . . barren. Well, maybe not technically barren, but I might as well have been. Here it was, Christmas Eve, and I should be home helping my own kids make Christmas cookies. But instead, I could only spend the day looking into the windows of other people's lives, a silent witness to their good fortune.

All I wanted to do was go home and climb into bed, but when I looked at the clock, it was only two. I still had hours left and I needed something to do to kill time while I waited for everyone else to trickle in. So, I made cupcakes. That might sound a little odd, but when I'm sad, I make cupcakes.

Ever since I was a little girl, when I had a bad day at school or my pet goldfish died or I failed a test, I made cupcakes with my mom. She dragged out the tins and the pastel paper liners and we went to work. This ritual continued into my adult life, marking such auspicious occasions as dropping out of college (temporarily) and more than one broken engagement. When my parents moved away, my mother gave me a box filled with everything I would need to carry on the tradition, should the need arise. There's just something about eating a cupcake that cheers people up and makes them feel cared for. They're pretty, they're almost impossible to screw up, and you can eat the whole thing without feeling too guilty.

I quickly whipped up a batch, sliding them into the oven just in time as the bell announced another customer. "I'll be right with you," I shouted from the kitchen.

"It's all right, dear. Take your time."

When I emerged from the back, I was happy to see an elderly woman with blue hair and a bright purple coat, standing at the counter.

"Mrs. Forbes! I was afraid you weren't coming this year."

"Mr. Forbes and I just got back from Colorado yesterday. That last storm slowed us up a bit. I was afraid we were going to be spending Christmas in the airport. How have you been?"

"I've been just fine, thank you. If you wait here, I have

something for you in the back." I disappeared into the kitchen to collect her customary order.

✳ ✳✳ ✳ ✳ ✳ ✳

Mrs. Forbes only comes to the bakery once a year, at Christmastime. She and her ninety-year-old husband spend most of the year traveling, but they always come home for the holidays because Mr. Forbes loves fruitcake.

The year I opened the bakery, she came in at the beginning of December, asking if I sold fruitcakes. I've never been a huge fan of fruitcake, and I only bake things I like. I told her that she was the first person who'd ever been interested and that I didn't even have a recipe. She reached into her coat pocket and produced a worn 3x5 card, penciled in elegant handwriting. She told me it was her own recipe and that she'd made it every year since she married her husband, fifty-one years ago. As she slid the paper across the counter, I could see that her hands were bent and twisted. She lamented that her arthritis had gotten so much worse this year, she was afraid she wouldn't be able to manage it. Her husband, Lamont, was just crazy about fruitcake, and she hated to disappoint him. I took the recipe and told her that I would do my best. She promised to come back a week before Christmas to collect her treasure.

I was so nervous about the task with which I'd been entrusted; I didn't dare leave it to chance. I went to the store and bought the ingredients right away for a trial run. I even had to make a special trip to the liquor store for a bottle of bourbon. Mrs. Forbes' instructions regarding the exact quantities of the liquor were a little vague, so I asked the man at the register exactly how much a splash was. I was rewarded with a blank stare and a request to see my ID, so I had to use my own judgment.

Since I don't drink, I'd never even considered cooking with alcohol, but Mrs. Forbes opened my eyes. I found a great recipe for a chocolate rum cake that people go nuts over. I even took it to a church dinner once—it won the blue ribbon. One envious woman asked what my secret ingredient was, and I told her it was love. (With a straight face, no less.)

I must have made the fruitcake four times before I decided it was worthy. My grandmother agreed to be my taster, since I really had no frame of reference as far as fruitcake was concerned. The first batch was too dry, the second too boozy, the third too gummy. But she pronounced the fourth batch to be just right, like an aged Goldilocks. I knew it must be okay when she asked me to leave the rest of the loaf. I nervously made the final batch and waited for Mrs. Forbes to return.

She arrived right before closing time, a few days before Christmas. I brought the loaves back from where they were hidden in the kitchen, and my heart was racing. I felt like a kid, presenting my science project for scrutiny and hoping to win first prize. She carefully opened the twist tie to release the aroma, sniffing delicately inside the bag. I hovered near the counter, waiting anxiously as she contemplated.

"This looks delicious, dear, and it smells even better. Lamont will be so pleased." She took her wallet from her purse, but I put my hand over hers.

"I can't take your money."

"But I want to pay you. You went to all this trouble," she said, obviously confused.

"I don't even know if it's any good. You take it home and let your husband try it first; see what he thinks."

"Well, if you insist." She thanked me again and went home, and for a few days I wondered what had happened. But with all the craziness of the holidays, I soon forgot about Mr. and Mrs. Forbes.

The day after Christmas, they returned. The two of them shuffled through the door together and I couldn't help smiling when I noticed that they moved the same way—slowly, hunched over like two question marks.

"How nice to see you, Mrs. Forbes. This must be your

husband I've heard so much about."

I put out my hand for him to shake, and he took it firmly. He smelled of Old Spice, evoking a pang of nostalgia for my own grandfather. "And that would make you Miss Abbie."

"Guilty as charged," I admitted, my cheeks pink with delight at the thought of being Miss Abbie.

"I believe we have an account to settle with you, young lady." He took a fifty-dollar bill from his pocket and pressed it into my palm.

"This is far too much," I protested.

"It's all right—I can afford it," he said, his eyes sparkling. "Besides, it just wouldn't have been Christmas without fruit-cake."

"Well, you're very generous. Thank you very much."

"I'll see you next year?" Mrs. Forbes asked, more a question than a statement, like a child asking permission for a treat.

"I wouldn't miss it."

They made their slow procession to the door when suddenly, Mr. Forbes paused. He left his wife where she was, coming back to the counter.

"Don't tell Margie, but I think your fruitcake is even better than hers," he whispered, leaning close to my ear.

I grinned. "It will be our little secret," I whispered back.

He rejoined Mrs. Forbes, and they continued their trek to the door. I watched as he reached for her gnarled hand, taking it comfortably in his.

✳ ✳ ✳ ✳ ✳ ✳ ✳

I deposited the fruitcake on the counter in front of Mrs. Forbes, and she gave me her customary fifty dollars, with Mr. Forbes's compliments. We talked for a minute until more people started to arrive. As she thanked me again, I heard the timer buzzing in the kitchen.

"Would you like a cupcake?" I asked her. "They're just coming out of the oven. I could send two—one for you and one for Mr. Forbes," I said temptingly.

"That's sweet, but I really have to get home. I have some pork chops in the Crock Pot, and besides, I'm sure Lamont will only have eyes for fruitcake tonight."

I took the cupcakes out of the oven, putting them on a tray to cool. After I helped the customers, I slathered the cupcakes with cream cheese frosting before dusting them with coconut, like sweet snowflakes. I barely had them settled in the case before my last customers of the day snatched them up. They were headed up to a cabin to spend their holidays skiing, and they wanted something sugary to look forward to when they took a break from the slopes. I gave them a good deal because it was Christmas Eve; I wouldn't be open tomorrow, and I didn't want them to go to waste.

The last boxes of cookies were safely in the arms of their owners and my cupcakes had a home, so I locked the door and turned the sign from open to closed. I had one stop to make on my way home.

Three

As I drove to my sister's house, Frank Sinatra sang "Have Yourself a Merry Little Christmas," making me feel even more dejected. But I brushed the feelings away. It was Christmas Eve, and I was determined to be cheerful. On the seat next to me rested the last box of Santa cookies, reserved for my nieces and nephew. Morgan is the oldest—she's nine, then Jake, who is seven, and the last is Hannah, who is five. They all have their own distinct personalities. Morgan is quiet, and you'd never notice her delicate features because her head is always buried in a book. Jake is all boy except for his impossibly long eyelashes, and he delights in tormenting his sisters mercilessly. And Hannah has golden, curly hair and never stops talking— she's quite possibly the smartest five-year-old I've ever met. I can't imagine loving them more if they were mine.

The front door was unlocked, so I knocked and went right in. "Hello?" I called out.

"Over here, Aunt Abbie," a little voice announced.

I walked into the living room where I found Hannah sprawled by the fireplace, concentrating on something she was writing. She paused, her little brow wrinkled thoughtfully. "How do you spell *bicycle*?" she asked.

I sat down next to her and showed her how to write it. "Is this your Christmas list?"

"Yup."

"I thought you guys already did them online."

"We did, but I'm not really sure how much I trust the computer. I mean, what if there's a big storm and Santa's Internet goes down? Or what if his computer breaks? I want something real that Santa can touch, in case anything goes wrong," she said seriously.

I kissed her on the forehead. "I don't blame you. It never hurts to cover all your bases."

She noticed the box I was carrying. "Are those the cookies?" she whispered, her eyes bright.

I nodded. "It's probably almost time to put them out for Santa and head for bed. Should we go get the milk?"

Hannah stood up, taking my hand and leading me into the kitchen. Jack was standing in the open refrigerator door, his head back as he casually chugged the rest of the milk straight from the gallon jug. I smacked him on the arm.

"Daddy!" Hannah wailed.

He wiped his mouth with the back of his hand. "What?"

"You just drank Santa's milk!"

Realization dawned on his face. "Sweetie, I'm sorry. I didn't think about it." He scanned the contents of the fridge. "Maybe Santa would like some juice this year instead. Or a Diet Coke—he is getting kind of fat."

"Dad, he's supposed to be fat; he's Santa!" She sighed heavily. "This is a disaster. No one leaves cookies and juice."

"It's all right, Hannah Banana. We'll go out and find some more milk. Grab your coat." She scampered off to the closet, and Jack gave me an apologetic look.

"Thanks, Abbie. I guess I owe you one."

Hannah reappeared in her coat, and I noticed she was wearing footie pajamas. I frowned. "Where are your shoes?"

She shrugged. "I could only find ones that didn't match."

"I bet they still keep your feet warm though."

"My feet are okay. You can carry me to the car."

I picked her up and headed toward the front door. "You're

getting so big I can hardly lift you anymore. Maybe you should have a Diet Coke."

She giggled. "I don't like Diet Coke."

"Me neither."

We drove around for a while, looking for a store that was still open, but the only place we could find was a 7-11.

"I want to pick the milk," she announced when we got inside. I put her down, and she ran straight to the cooler. The man at the counter watched with amusement as she struggled to open the door and then stood on tiptoes, trying to reach the milk.

"You have to have milk for Santa, right?" I said, by way of explanation.

"Believe it or not, you aren't the first ones tonight who left it until the last minute, and you probably won't be the last."

"Well, it wasn't exactly like that. We did have milk, but someone drank it."

Hannah deposited the carton on the counter. "Daddy drank it." She looked up at me expectantly. "Can I have a Slurpee?"

"I think we'd better skip it—it's pretty late."

"Pleeeeease?" she begged.

I caved. "Just get the smallest one. And hurry; we've got to get you home before Santa gets there."

She ran to the back and started perusing her choices. I cleared my throat, smiling. "This must be a bummer, having to work on Christmas Eve."

He returned my smile. "It's all right. I'm divorced, and we didn't have any kids, so I guess I'm not really missing anything. I kind of like being out with other people. It beats sitting in my apartment alone, you know?"

I nodded. I could definitely understand where he was coming from. I noticed that his hair was graying at the edges and I wondered how long he'd been divorced. When I looked back, Hannah was still deep in thought, weighing the benefits of one Slurpee over another, agonizing over her choice.

"Hannah, sweetie, we have to get you to bed. Please just pick one! This is not the last Slurpee you'll ever have."

"I'm almost ready."

"I like the white one," I said.

She wrinkled up her nose. "Eeeeewww."

"I don't care which one you get, as long as you choose right now. I'm going to count to three . . ."

That seemed to spur her into action. She put her cup up to the nozzle and pulled it decisively.

"Do you need any help?" I called out.

"I can do it," she said as the machine spluttered, the Slurpee lurching over the edge of the cup.

"She's a cutie," the clerk commented, and something between pride and pain surged through me when I realized that he assumed she was mine. Hannah finally made her appearance, sampling her Slurpee with the spoon-end of the straw. He gave me the total, and I pulled out a few bills and some change. I wished him a Merry Christmas, and I scooped up Hannah and hurried to the car.

"You'd better get busy with that Slurpee. You have to finish it before we get back," I said, buckling her in.

"Why?"

"Because Jake and Morgan would feel bad."

By the time we got back to the house, Hannah was sucking loudly on her straw, trying to get every last bit of syrup that might be lingering in the bottom of her cup. I left the evidence in the car, but when I picked her up, I was dismayed to notice her popsicle-red lips and tongue. I tried unsuccessfully to wipe it from the corners of her mouth.

"Your mom's going to have a fit," I said as we came through the door.

Hannah carried the milk into the kitchen where she poured it into a tall glass with much concentration, careful not to spill a drop. I couldn't help thinking how funny it was: with the milk she's extra cautious, but give her a Slurpee, and she's a train wreck.

Just then, Grace appeared in the doorway, hands on her hips.

"Sorry," I said sheepishly. "It took us forever to find someplace that was still open."

She glared at me. "Because it's Christmas, I'm going to ignore that blatantly obvious Slurpee moustache. Did you really think you were going to get away with that? I can see it across the room."

Hannah whispered to me, in a voice that carried through the kitchen. "Next time I promise I'll get the white one." She walked slowly to the little table by the tree where the cookies were, balancing the too-full milk glass in her little hands.

I could tell that Grace was trying to keep a stern expression, but she couldn't help cracking up at Hannah's last remark. She rolled her eyes, but I could tell she wasn't too mad at me. "Honestly, it's Christmas Eve, it's going to be murder getting her into bed anyway, and you have to pump her full of sugar."

"I know, I know. What can I say—I've never made any secret of the fact that I couldn't say no to them."

"Thanks for going to get the milk, even if you are sadly lacking in backbone."

"No problem."

There was a commotion coming from the living room. Morgan and Jake had joined Hannah by the tree, where she'd placed her list prominently next to the milk and cookies.

"Why did you make another letter? We did them already, remember?" Jake said, crossing his arms in front of his chest.

"I want mine right here next to the tree, so Santa can double-check my presents," Hannah explained.

"Whatever. People do all the important stuff on the computer now. Don't you know anything?"

"Jacob!" Grace said sharply. "You'd better be nice to your sister. I could still put in a bad report with Santa."

Jake was undeterred. "It's too late, Mom. The sleigh is packed."

"I have his phone number on speed dial."

"He's already left the North Pole," he shot back.

"It's a cell phone number."

Jake looked momentarily thrown by this never-before-considered possibility. If Santa had the Internet, he was bound to have a cell phone. "Sorry, Hannah," he said finally, staring at the ground as he kicked at the tassels on the rug.

"That's better. Maybe it's time to go to bed now. It's much easier to be good when you're asleep," Grace said. "Say good night to Aunt Abbie."

"Can't we stay up a little longer?" they begged in unison.

I put a hand to my ear, pretending to listen closely. "What's that noise I hear on the roof? Is that reindeer hooves?" I said. The kids squealed, stampeding up the stairs in the direction of their bedrooms, but Morgan stopped suddenly.

"Why is Hannah's mouth all red?" she asked suspiciously.

"It's a rash."

"Does she have germs?"

"She's not contagious. I'm pretty sure it will be gone in the morning."

Morgan looked relieved. "Good night, Aunt Abbie."

Hannah came back, planting a quick kiss on my cheek.

"Thanks for taking me to get the milk."

"You're welcome, sweetie. Now get to bed, or Santa won't come. I'll see you tomorrow." She disappeared quickly, off to dream of sugar plums or whatever kids dream about now. In the distance, I could barely hear Jake's voice.

"Hey, that's not a rash . . ."

Grace smiled. "It really was nice of you, going out for milk at this hour."

"Well, we can't have poor Hannah up there lying awake, worrying about Daddy drinking all the milk and how she won't get any presents because Santa really isn't a Diet Coke kind of guy."

Jack came around the corner, his mouth full of one of the iced Christmas cookies. "Yeah. The ironic thing is I'm going to drink that milk too."

Grace punched him in the arm. "What are you doing? The kids might see you—they just went upstairs!"

Jack pointed at his T-shirt. "Am I wearing a sign today that says, 'All women: please feel free to physically abuse me'?"

"I have no problem with you eating the cookies, *Santa*, but you could at least wait until the kids are asleep," Grace hissed. "Do you really want to have the 'There is no Santa' conversation tonight?"

"No, dear," he said, forcing a smile. "I'll lay off the cookies for a while. It's just hard because they're SO GOOD." He made sad puppy-dog-eyes in my general direction.

"Don't try to butter her up," Grace said.

"It's too late. He always knows what to say to be forgiven."

He grinned before shoving the rest of the cookie into his mouth. "See?" he mumbled.

I giggled. Even Grace couldn't help laughing, her patented scolding look dissolving in an instant.

"Well, I'd better get home," I said, moving toward the door. "Are you going to bed soon?"

"We have a little bit of wrapping left, but I should be asleep just in time for one of the kids to wake me up so we can open presents. It's an exercise in futility. By the way, did you get your letter off to Santa?" she asked.

"It must have been the futility part that made you think of that."

"No, seriously."

"I'm with Hannah on this one. I can't say in all honesty that I trust the Internet. I guess I'm just old-fashioned."

"It isn't too late, you know. I've got a pen and paper right here—"

"Good night, Grace," I said, opening the front door.

"I'll see you tomorrow night. If you get what you ask for, you're welcome to bring him to dinner."

I waved, closing the door and cutting her off before her imagination could carry her away completely.

Four

*⁕**⁕⁕**✳***⁕***⁕**✶**⁕**

I carefully made my way up the driveway to my house, trying to avoid slipping on the patches of ice. Although I couldn't see them, I knew they were there lurking, waiting to catch an unsuspecting victim. When I made it safely to the door, I went inside and plugged in the lights on my tree. The tree looked a little pathetic with only the one box from my parents, so I brought out the stuff for Morgan, Jake, and Hannah. That made it seem cheerier. I didn't bother to take off all my layers of winter padding, flopping instead into the armchair in my tiny living room. It was late and, despite my better judgment, I felt a bit silly.

Although the comfortable chair was beckoning me to stay, I forced myself to get up. I went into the kitchen and got a notepad and a pen from one of the drawers. Leaning over the counter, I composed a very short letter, grinning to myself like a little girl the whole time.

Dear Santa,

I've been a good girl this year. (Well ... pretty good.) I have a nice life and there's only one thing that I really want—one thing that's missing. If you happen to have an extra one lying around your

workshop, I would really like a husband. I promise
to take good care of him.
Love, Abbie

I tore out the letter and put it on the chair in the living room where I had been sitting. I began rummaging through my cupboards, looking for something cookie-like in nature to leave for Santa. Despite the fact that I owned a bakery, there were no cookies—homemade or otherwise—anywhere in my kitchen. I finally settled on a half-eaten tin of Pringles and a Coke. After all those cookies, Santa was bound to be craving something salty anyway. I put them on the chair, next to the letter.

Even though I knew that I was never supposed to leave the tree lights on at the risk of burning my house down, I couldn't help it. They looked so pretty in the window against the snow that was slowly beginning to fall outside. I took one last look before going down the hall to my room.

I finally managed to struggle out of the closet's worth of clothes I was wearing. I put on my pajamas and crawled under the covers. Even though I was an adult who knew that the chances of Santa shimmying down my chimney with a gift-wrapped man were about the same as my odds of winning the lottery, I couldn't help being a little bit excited. For a minute, I was a girl again, lying as still as I could under the covers and imagining that I could hear Santa's heavy boots on the roof, or the jingling of a bell.

I turned onto my side, pulling the blankets up underneath my chin and feeling my eyelids getting heavy. I smiled, thinking about what I would tell the people who asked what I got for Christmas. I allowed my eyes to drift closed, picturing myself introducing my gorgeous new present to all my family and friends . . .

✳ ✳ ✳ ✳ ✳ ✳ ✳

I awoke suddenly to a loud clunk that scared me so badly I immediately hid my head under the covers. I held my breath for a minute, wondering if I had dreamed the whole thing. After what seemed like hours of lying rigid in the darkness, straining to hear any other sounds, I glanced at the alarm clock. It was only 4:07 AM. What if the noise was my Christmas tree falling over? What if it had triggered a spark and my carpet was starting to smolder right now? Worse yet, what if there was someone in the house?

I threw off the covers and grabbed my bathrobe. I sneaked down the hallway, stopping in the kitchen to look for a make-shift weapon. I had some nice kitchen knives, but I didn't hon-estly think I could stab anyone; even the thought made me queasy. I grabbed a heavy rolling pin out of the drawer, and the weight felt comfortable in my hands. I could definitely club someone with it if I had to. I considered getting the fire extinguisher too, but I couldn't smell any smoke.

I proceeded toward the living room, stopping when I could see the familiar sight of the lights from the tree, reflect-ing in the glass. I froze for a second, puzzled. If the tree was still upright, then where had the noise come from? I hefted my rolling pin, ready to storm the living room. If there was someone in there, I had the element of surprise on my side, and I wasn't about to cower and wait for him to find me. My heart hammered in my chest, and I knew that if I thought about it too long, I would chicken out. I stepped out from my hiding place into plain sight, my trusty rolling pin at the ready.

At first glance, I couldn't see anything unusual, but as I stepped fully into the room, I could see something under the tree that wasn't there before.

Something . . . big.

I quietly inched toward the lump, and my breath caught in my throat as it moved slightly. Upon closer inspection, I determined that it was, in fact, breathing. I backed away until I was flat against the wall, trying not to hyperventilate as I decided what to do. I noticed for the first time that the chair was empty; the snacks and the letter were gone.

This couldn't be happening.

The lump on the floor snored, and I jumped. He shifted until I could see part of his face. He was definitely no one I knew, and he looked like someone I might find on the pages of a magazine, not the floor of my living room. He wore a long, dark coat over his pajamas, and his feet were hidden in plush slippers. I could see from his profile that he had strong features: a straight nose and good hair, and that little indentation men sometimes have in their chin. I moved closer, even as my head informed me that I should retreat immediately. I unconsciously reached out to touch his perfect chin, stopping myself at the last possible moment.

My rational mind took over. *Get a hold of yourself! You can't just pick him up and play with him!*

But he's what I asked for, I argued. *Santa couldn't have done a better job if I'd drawn him a picture.*

You don't really think Santa just stuffed him down your chimney, do you? You must have been a very good girl this year . . .

"Stop it," I snapped aloud, slapping one hand over my mouth after it was already too late. He stirred but didn't open his eyes. Luckily for me, he appeared to be a very heavy sleeper.

Maybe he's a robber, I thought, realizing how weak it sounded.

And he was just so exhausted that he decided he needed a quick nap? the voice said sarcastically.

Maybe he's homeless, I tried.

Yes, homeless people often wander around in expensive coats and slippers, it countered.

I shook my head firmly, as if I could physically dislodge the voice from my consciousness. It didn't really matter why he was here—I just knew he shouldn't be. The only way to find out how he got here was to ask him. I took a deep breath, leaned a little closer, and poked him tentatively with the end of the rolling pin. He didn't budge. I tried again, a little more forcefully this time. He rolled onto his side, turning his back to me. I lost patience, jabbing him in the ribs.

"Excuse me," I said, throwing in a few more pokes with the rolling pin for good measure.

He finally turned to face me, opening his eyes sleepily and wincing slightly from the repeated jabs.

"Hello," he said calmly, as if we were being introduced at a party.

"Well, hello to you too. Do you mind telling me what you're doing in my living room?" I said, as pleasantly as I could under the circumstances.

He looked momentarily confused, glancing around the room as if a quick surveillance of his surroundings would explain everything.

"I'm sorry, who are you?" His voice was soft and warm, like melted chocolate.

"I think I should be the one asking that question."

He looked around the room again. "Where am I?"

"I just told you. You're in my living room. Now it's your turn to answer a question."

"I'm afraid I can't," he said, rubbing his head like it was sore. His answer wasn't confrontational; simply a matter-of-fact statement.

"Are you on drugs or something?"

He shook his head. "I don't do drugs."

"Good for you. Now, I'm through kidding around. Who are you and what are you doing in my house?"

"I told you, I can't remember!" he said, the agitation finally beginning to register in his voice.

I decided to try another approach. I sat in the armchair, putting on my best smile. "Let's start with something simple, shall we? My name is Abbie. What's your name?"

"I don't know."

"Come on, you didn't even try."

"It's my *name*—I shouldn't *have* to try!" he exploded.

"All right, calm down. Check your pockets."

"Oh, that's right, I remember now. I keep my name on a slip of paper in my coat pocket in case I forget who I am."

"I thought you might find a wallet or an ID, smarty-pants."

He reached into one coat pocket, coming up empty. From the second pocket he pulled a large wad of cash, but nothing else. No keys, no credit cards, no ID. He looked up at me like he was lost.

"Are you sure you don't know who I am?" he asked finally.

"Well, I did ask Santa for a man for Christmas," I said bashfully. I thought that maybe this pathetic nugget of information might take his mind off of his own situation.

He raised one eyebrow in a way that I found incredibly sexy. "Really? I don't remember asking for a woman, though." He started rubbing his head again in a distracted way.

"Did you hit your head?" I asked, peeking at it. "Maybe that's why you're having trouble remembering things."

"I don't recall hitting my head."

"Maybe I should take a look?" I asked, scooting closer to him.

"Are you a doctor?"

"No, I'm a baker."

"Well then, by all means," he said, waving me toward him.

"Where does it hurt?" I started carefully massaging his scalp. He smelled clean, like soap.

"Actually, it doesn't hurt at all right now," he said, and I could feel the tension go out of his shoulders as he relaxed.

I stopped abruptly, blushing. "Well, I don't feel any bumps. Maybe there's another way we can jog your memory."

I might have been imagining it, but he seemed disappointed. "How are we going to do that?"

"I can ask you questions . . . like a game!"

"What kind of questions?"

"You know . . . mundane things that might trigger something more important. Are you hungry?"

A puzzled look crossed his features. "Is that one of the questions?"

"Of course not. I just thought you might want something to eat."

He looked out the window. "It's the middle of the night."

"It is not! Besides, I'm usually getting up about now."

"Are you insane?"

"I run a bakery."

"An all-night bakery?"

I rolled my eyes. "I have to get up early and bake so that the food is ready when I open."

"Why don't you just sleep in, sell the stuff from yesterday, and bake in the afternoon?"

I looked at him sternly. "Because I want everything to be just right. People come to my bakery because they know my stuff is cooked fresh every morning, and it makes them feel loved—like their mother cooked them breakfast."

"So, you're the surrogate mother to the neighborhood, huh? I wonder what a psychotherapist would say about that."

"It's an expression of love," I interjected. I wasn't sure I liked where this conversation was going, so I turned it around on him. "What about your mother? Did she make you breakfast?"

"I really couldn't say."

"Do you remember her name?"

He shook his head. He studied my face for a minute before giving me a wide grin.

"What?" I asked, unable to meet his direct stare.

"It's funny, but I wouldn't have pegged you as the big, hot breakfast sort. You seem more like the grab-what-you-can-on-the-way-out-the-door type. In fact, I'm getting a very strong cold cereal vibe right now."

I walked to the cupboard above the fridge, pulling it open

to reveal eight different boxes of cereal.

"I knew it!" he crowed. "So, you have the overwhelming need to take care of everyone you know, but you end up neglecting yourself in the process."

"I happen to like cereal, Mr. Freud. So, what's it gonna be?"

"I'll have bacon and eggs."

"I have cereal. And toast."

"I think I'll stick with the toast. If I had to choose from that many cereals, I'd be here all morning."

"Toast it is." I pulled two pieces of bread out of the bag and slid them into the toaster slots, pushing down the lever. "I like hot chocolate with my toast. Can I get you some?"

"That sounds nice."

While I was waiting for the water to boil, I started thinking about the strangeness of the last thirty minutes. I was in my bathrobe, making breakfast for a stranger in *his* bathrobe, and the thing that worried me the most was that something about it felt really right. It was almost like we'd been married for years, having toast and cocoa and chatting. I had my back to the guy, but I swear I could feel his eyes burning a hole in it. I resisted the urge to turn around because I needed a minute to think.

All the signs pointed toward the same conclusion: Santa Claus came down my chimney, read my note, commiserated, ate my Pringles, and drank my Coke, and then left me what I had been fruitlessly searching for my entire life. Too bad the aforementioned scenario was impossible . . .

Wasn't it?

The smoke pouring out of the toaster brought me out of my daydream. I pushed up the lever and the toast jumped out, completely charred. If I hadn't been so lost in thought, I probably would have heard the bread screaming. I looked over my shoulder to see him watching me in amusement.

"The lever sticks," I said, coughing as I fanned the smoke away, hoping it wouldn't set off the fire alarm.

"Why don't you just get a new toaster?"

"Because this one works fine; it just needs a little super-vision." I threw the blackened toast in the garbage, putting two new slices into the toaster. I chided myself for the little unrealistic fantasy I'd been indulging in. It didn't matter if Santa brought him or if he was a burglar or if he simply appeared out of thin air. Since I had conveniently detached myself from romance in general, he was no concern of mine. The best thing I could do now was focus on figuring out where to return him. I popped up the toast, placing the nicely browned slices on plates.

"See?" I said. "Perfect." I spread butter on the hot toast, watching it melt into the crevices, feeling more in control. "So, butter or margarine?" I said briskly.

"Whatever you have is fine."

"I meant, are you a butter person or a margarine person?"

"Oh, I get it. We're starting with the questions now. I would have to say butter."

"Me too. Margarine is disgusting. Coke or Pepsi?"

"Pepsi."

"Dog or cat?"

"Definitely dog."

"Republican or Democrat?"

"I think that discussing religion or politics can only get you into trouble."

I spooned the cocoa into the hot water. "For a guy who can't remember his name, you're pretty quick with all the other answers."

He smiled. "You haven't asked me any hard questions yet."

"Since you brought up religion—"

"Next question, please."

"Are you married?"

"I have no idea," he replied smoothly.

"Let's be realistic," I was suddenly feeling a little angry, and I wasn't sure if I was angry with him or just myself for initiating this little game. It seemed like a good idea in the first place, but then, so had asking Santa for a man. "You obviously came from somewhere, judging from your attire. And good-looking guys like you don't just drop out of the sky, so you must belong to someone. We just have to figure out where you came from so we can return you to your rightful owner."

"You make me sound like a pair of gloves. Did I hear you say I was good-looking?"

My cheeks colored furiously. "No!"

"So I just imagined it?'

"I was just . . . thinking aloud," I said, completely flustered now.

"Its okay to say you like me. I won't tell anyone."

"I don't even know you. Besides, telling someone they're good-looking and saying you like them are two very different things. One is merely an observation."

"And the other?" he said, his head cocked to the side in a way that I was trying not to find adorable.

"I don't like anyone. At least, not like that."

"Just so we're clear, are you married? Because that last answer could really go either way."

I smiled in spite of myself. "That would be a hearty no."

"Do I detect a note of bitterness in that answer?"

"You can take it however you want."

"If you had given me a simple no, that would be something. But there must be a story behind a hearty no."

"You first."

"I'm hardly in a position to be regaling you with stories from my life, so you will have to do the honors."

"Let's just say that I've come to accept that the right guy just isn't out there—not for me, anyway."

"They say that there's someone for everyone. Why should you be the exception?"

Suddenly it was like something just clicked. "Grace," I muttered under my breath.

He quickly put his toast back on the plate. "I'm sorry. We can say grace, if you want to."

"I meant my *sister* Grace. She sent you here, didn't she?"

"I couldn't swear to it, but I don't think I know anyone named Grace."

"What about Jack—Jack Walker? He's my brother-in-law. Maybe you work with him."

"What does he do?"

"He's in advertising."

He closed his eyes tightly, as if he was trying to think hard. "Doesn't ring a bell."

"It has to be Grace. This is exactly like something she would do. She's forever trying to set me up, but this is going a little too far."

"Why are you so sure your sister did this?"

"She's the only one with a key, and as far as I can tell, there are no broken windows or locks. Unless . . ."

"Unless what?"

"Well, I do have this tendency to forget to lock the front door. But I'm almost positive that I checked it before I went to bed."

"The world we live in is too scary not to lock your doors; anyone could wander in," he said innocently. "Besides, maybe there's another way in here."

"Really? And just how else would you get in here?"

"I don't know. Maybe . . . the chimney?" He took off his coat, hanging it over a chair.

"Oh, that's hilarious," I deadpanned. "No, this little scheme has Grace written all over it." My eyes went immediately to his pajama top.

His *monogrammed* pajama top. 'SBC,' it proclaimed in neat, white letters.

I pointed to it. "Look! A clue! Do you know what it stands for?"

He examined it, deep in thought. "Wait a second; I've got it! I don't know why I didn't think of it earlier."

"So you know who you are? That's wonderful!"

"It makes perfect sense. I arrived at your house on Christmas Eve, and my initials are SBC. . . ." He paused to let these tidbits of information sink in, but I still had no idea where he was going with it. "Do I have to spell it out for you? I am Santa Claus!" he announced triumphantly.

I stared at him. "Santa B. Claus? What does the B stand for?"

"I don't know. Beauregard?"

"Riiight."

"Trust me, if your middle name was Beauregard, you wouldn't advertise it either."

I giggled. "I don't really think that's what the initials stand for, do you?"

"I guess we'll just have to wait to see if the elves report me missing."

"Now that's an idea . . ." I said, jumping up and grabbing the phone book from the drawer. I flipped through the pages feverishly, searching for the right entry.

"I'm pretty sure Santa has an unlisted number."

I gave him a withering look. "I'm trying to find the number for the police station. Maybe someone has already called, looking for you. It's worth a shot."

I dialed the number and spoke to a very nice officer who informed me that no one had been reported missing who matched that description. He suggested that I bring my John Doe in so that they could get a picture of him for the paper. Since he was in his pajamas, the officer was fairly certain he was local and couldn't have gotten far on foot.

We got into the car and drove to the police station. They took his fingerprints and ran them through their database, but didn't come up with any matches. So at least I knew he wasn't a criminal. Not one who'd been caught, anyway. They took a couple of pictures of him and promised to circulate them, and I gave them my phone number to call if they had any leads.

We walked outside to discover the day had begun without

us. It was officially Christmas, and a white one at that. The sun apparently had decided to make a cameo appearance, making the snow-covered trees and fences seem brighter. The streets were almost empty since everyone was inside opening presents, except the few desperate parents out looking for a convenience store that wasn't sold out of the one thing they'd forgotten to buy—batteries.

"Wow. What a beautiful day," he commented, as if we were suddenly sharing the same brain.

"Yeah, it's nice to see the sun for a change." We stood there on the steps of the police station, and I searched my mind frantically for something to say. We didn't seem to have any problems making conversation before, but suddenly we were strangers. For the first time since I found him, we'd come to a standstill. I looked at him out of the corner of my eye and was even more distressed to see him watching me, like he was waiting for me to take the lead. The voice in my head added to the pressure by hinting that everything hinged on what happened next.

"So . . ." I said slowly, hoping that he would take the opening and run with it.

"Yes . . . exactly. What now?"

"I guess the next logical step would be to find you some-place to stay."

He squinted against the blinding sunlight. "I was thinking maybe we should go sledding."

"I would have to say that, right now, getting you a bed for the night is a little more pressing."

"But it's a perfect day for it," he protested. "I saw a great hill on our way over here."

"Honestly, you sound like my nephew, Jake." I dragged him toward the car. "You'll thank me for this tonight when you're not curled up on a bench in the park."

"I wish I had some real clothes to wear. I don't suppose they come with the hotel room."

"I doubt it. I'm afraid you'll just have to make do with the pajamas today; its Christmas and none of the stores are open."

"Never mind, it's still early. There will be plenty of time to go sledding after we get the hotel room."

"I don't know if sledding is such a great idea," I hedged.

"Now, the most important thing in a relationship is compromise. So, first we do something you want to do, and then it's my turn to choose."

"Really? And where did you get that bit of homespun wisdom?"

"I'm pretty sure I remember reading it somewhere. Now, let's get your thing over with so we can move onto the fun part."

"Unfortunately, there's a gaping hole in your plan."

"Which is . . . ?"

"We can't go sledding because I don't have a sled."

"Yes, you do. I saw it in your house."

"Where?" I said, bewildered.

"In your living room, by the tree."

"You mean the one with the bow on it?"

He snapped his fingers. "Exactly."

"It's a Christmas present."

"For me? You shouldn't have."

"It's for my nephew and nieces."

"We'll be really careful with it. When we're finished, I'll put the bow back on and they'll never know the difference."

"We're not going sledding, and that's final."

"Then I'm sleeping on your couch until we figure out who I am."

Five

The sled was perched precariously at the top of the highest hill in town. I suddenly felt dizzy, and I wasn't sure if it was from the lack of oxygen at this height or the grueling climb to reach the top. I was trying very hard to breathe normally so as not to seem like an out-of-shape gopher, plucked from hibernation and taken on a forced march. Although I was winded, I made a point of grinning like I was having the time of my life.

The hill had been recently divided into chunks and sold as lots for new homes, which would be built in the spring. The trees had already been cleared, making it the perfect spot for any kid within miles with a sled. It was a dream come true for all sledders . . . and my personal nightmare.

"Well, what are you waiting for?" he said, patting the seat behind him. He'd taken the front seat, for which I was grateful, but I was still contemplating how difficult it would be to bail at the last minute, leaving him to make the perilous journey by himself. I reluctantly slid onto the back, feeling my anxiety reach a new level as we teetered on the edge of oblivion. "Ready?" he said, putting a hand down to give us a push.

"No, no! Wait!" I yelped.

"What is it?"

"This is a bad idea."

"It'll be great, you'll see. It looks scary now, but after the first run, you'll be dragging me up the hill to go again."

"I don't feel safe."

"Put your arms around me."

I tentatively snaked my arms around his chest, holding on tightly and burying my face in his neck. "Just tell me when it's over."

"Don't worry about me," he croaked. "I don't really need to breathe."

I loosened up a little. "Sorry. Is that better?"

"Much. Okay, I'm going to count to three. One . . . two—"

"No! Not yet!"

He craned his head around so he could see me. "Now what?"

"Since we're about to die together, I need a name to call you."

"If we're going to die, does it really matter?"

I gave him a dirty look. "You need a name."

"All right, then, pick one."

"I thought maybe you already had one in mind. You must have been thinking about it." I was stalling for time, and he knew it.

"Nope. It's up to you."

"Well, this is a big deal. You can't just pick the first thing that comes to your mind."

"Yes, you can."

"Let's see . . ."

"Abbie, at the rate we're going we really will die here . . . from *old age*."

"Ben," I said, the name slipping from my lips before I even knew what was happening.

"Ben it is," he replied, pushing us off into the great, white unknown.

I screamed.

✳ ✳✳ ✴ ✳ ✳ ✳

We sat in hard, orange plastic chairs in the waiting area of the emergency room. Well, at least one of us did. I was in a wheelchair, my left foot resting on Ben's leg, cradled by the ice pack they gave me when we checked in. On the television in the corner, Jimmy Stewart was discovering what life would have been like if he'd never been born.

"I've never seen *It's a Wonderful Life* all the way through," I said, my own voice sounding strange to my ears through the pain-filled haze. "Everybody should see it at least once—it's a classic. And every year I tell myself I'm going to watch the whole thing, but something comes up and I never do."

"My leg's getting cold," Ben said.

I glared at him. "Whose fault is it we're here?"

"Mine," he said, his eyes on the floor.

"And how much trouble are you in?"

"A lot." His voice was full of penitence, but I could see now why he was so careful to direct his eyes away from mine.

"You're laughing!"

"I am not!"

"You are too—I can see it in your eyes. On the inside, you're practically doubled over with laughter."

He smiled widely at me as though I'd given him permission. "I can't help it. I keep picturing you, flying off the sled. Admit it; before we crashed, you were having a good time."

"I wasn't having a good time. I was terrified. And you're going to explain to my nieces and nephews why they're not getting a sled this year."

"I carried you up the hill. I couldn't get the sled too."

"I meant because it was in three pieces!"

"Which is perfect, since there are three of them."

"Besides, it's too dangerous. I don't know what I was thinking." They'd given me some Tylenol when I checked in, but it barely put a dent in my throbbing ankle and I was feeling more irritable by the minute. "I notice you escaped without as much as a scrape."

"Because I was relaxed, whereas every muscle in your body was all tensed up. You're lucky you didn't break your neck."

"My point exactly."

"Miss Canfield?"

"Yes?" we said in unison.

"We're ready to take you back now."

Ben pushed my wheelchair down the hall, chatting pleasantly with the nurse. She was very petite, nearly drowning in her size-extra-small scrubs with her blonde hair pulled into a messy knot. She seemed to think everything he said was amusing, and by the time we got to the room, they were laughing like old friends. It must have been the pain, but her giggle was so annoying that I wanted to beat her senseless with the clipboard she was holding.

"Your boyfriend is so cute," she gushed, as if Ben weren't in the room.

"I'm glad you approve. Maybe you can go sledding with him next time."

She giggled again like that was the funniest thing she'd ever heard, turning her attention to him and fluttering her eyelashes coyly. "Seriously, you don't happen to have a brother, do you?"

"Well, that's the trouble, you see. I can't remember."

She punched him on the shoulder lightly. "Are you teasing me?"

He shrugged his shoulders. "I have amnesia," he said, almost apologetically.

She gasped. "No. Way. That's amazing. You know, I read this article once—"

"Excuse me," I interrupted, my voice full of pent-up crankiness. "I know this is fascinating, but right now, could we concentrate on my foot? It really hurts."

"I'm sorry," she said, as if she'd just remembered there was someone else in the room. "Did they give you anything when you got here?"

"Just some Tylenol."

"If you had to rate your pain on a scale of one to ten, with ten being the worst pain you've ever been in, where would you say you're at now?"

"Eleven."

"O-kay," she chirped. "I'm going to see if we can't bump you up in the line for x-ray, and in the meantime, we'll get you something a little stronger. Are you allergic to anything?"

"Just sledding," I said, gritting my teeth.

She gave me a courtesy laugh, her eyes on Ben the entire time. "I'll be back in just a minute."

"Thank you," he said sincerely, flashing her a smile.

"Would you like me to leave the room when she comes back, so you two can get better acquainted?"

"Hey, that little display was solely for your benefit."

"Why? Do you think I need a crash course in flirting?"

"Nah. She likes me now, so she'll probably give you some morphine to knock you out so we can talk."

"I suppose I should thank you," I said, the sarcasm rolling off me in waves.

"Don't mention it."

✳ ✳ ✳ ✳ ✳ ✳ ✳

Ben wheeled me to the car. He tried to lift me into the seat, but I shrugged him off.

"I can do it myself."

"Just trying to be a gentleman," he said, stowing my crutches in the back seat.

I managed to wedge my giant foot with the boot on it into the car without causing myself too much additional pain. I still felt a little woozy from the shot they'd given me.

"How's the foot? Is your drug holiday holding out?" He slid easily into the driver's seat.

"How could something hurt that much and not be broken?"

"Sometimes a sprain hurts more than a break."

"And I'm guessing you've done both."

"Oh, lots of times," he said airily.

"How would you know if you've ever broken a bone? For all you know, you could be one of those people who are afraid to even leave the house."

Ben gave me a confident, almost smug look. "I don't think so. Besides, where do you think I learned how to get the good drugs?"

"I've never been in the emergency room in my life, and after half a day with you, I'm in pieces."

"Yeah, I've been meaning to tell you. I'm really sorry about the whole sledding incident. You didn't want to do it in the first place, and I should have listened to you."

I softened the tiniest bit. "It's all right. I didn't want to admit it, but I was sort of having an okay time. You know, before we crashed. But that doesn't mean I want to do it again," I said quickly.

"Well, I guess I better get you home."

"No, I have to get to my sister's house. I'm already late for dinner."

"I'll drive you there. I can walk to the hotel."

"I've got a better idea."

Six

"I'm not sure this is such a good plan," Ben said nervously as he parked in front of Grace's house.

"It's Christmas. You can't be alone."

"Yeah, but Christmas is family time. This is kind of intrusive."

"You think *this* is intrusive!" I said. "How about planting a man under your sister's tree because you think she's incapable of finding her own? I can't wait to see the look on their faces. They should be ashamed of themselves."

Ben shook his head. "I'm a little confused here. Didn't you say you asked Santa for a man?"

"I was actually hoping that you might have forgotten I said that."

"My life before I woke up in your living room is a blur, but everything since then is crystal clear."

"Lucky me."

"I still don't get why this makes you so angry. It seems like you would be happy that your sister somehow arranged for you to get what you wanted."

"That's not the reason I'm angry."

He threw his hands in the air. "You've lost me completely."

"I'm not angry because she brought you here; I'm angry

44

because she tricked me into thinking I wanted you in the first place."

"Well, I have to say that's not exactly flattering."

"I'm sorry. I know how that must have sounded. I shouldn't be taking my frustration out on you; you're as much the victim here as I am."

"But that's what I still don't understand. Unless they picked me up at a mental asylum, I must have agreed to this whole arrangement."

"I'm not sure I know where you're going with this."

"It doesn't make any sense. What happened between the time I was dropped off at your house and when I woke up?"

"Maybe you got hurt somehow. Maybe you hit your head and couldn't remember what the plan was, so they panicked and tried to dump you!"

"Unless your sister and brother-in-law are in the mafia, I think you might be getting a little carried away with that whole scenario."

"Well, it had to be them. They must have taken my letter to Santa too; how embarrassing. I'm sure Jack had a good laugh over it while he was wolfing down the Pringles."

"What Pringles?"

"I didn't have any cookies, so I left Santa some Pringles."

"Oh, right. Of course," Ben said, trying to stifle a laugh behind his hand.

"We'd better get in there—we're late enough as it is."

"I can't just show up unannounced."

"It's okay; I have a feeling they're expecting you. Anyway, Grace just has to learn that if she wants to play Santa, she'd better be prepared to deal with the consequences."

"And if you're wrong?"

"Then Santa really did bring you and I'm sure you'll be forgiven for coming to dinner, in light of the extraordinary circumstances."

We walked to the front door. I struggled with my awkward crutches, and we both shivered in the chilly night air.

The plastic grips on the bottom of my crutches were no match for the snow and ice. Every step was potentially treacherous, and more than once I caught myself starting to slide.

"I could always carry you," Ben offered gallantly.

"Don't even think about it. We're going to be a strange enough spectacle as it is."

Ben pulled his coat more tightly around him. "Speaking of which, I feel ridiculous wearing my pajamas."

"Well, I'm not exactly loving the crutches and boot either." I rang the doorbell, and we waited.

Jack opened the door. "Merry Christmas, Abbie. What happened to your foot?"

"That's all you can say? What happened to your foot?"

"I was just trying to be considerate."

"And my foot was really the first thing that caught your attention?"

"Oh, you mean the dude in his pajamas," he said grinning. "Where are my manners? Who's your friend?"

"Like you don't know," I shot back.

"Should I?"

"That's an excellent question, Jack."

"Honey, Abbie's here," Jack yelled into the house.

"Well, let her *in*!" she shouted back in an exasperated tone.

"I think you better come out here."

Jack was having way too much fun with this. I was more convinced than ever that they were the culprits. I could hear Grace's voice before I actually saw her.

"About time you got here. I've got a surprise for you. I guess Santa accidentally delivered your present to the wrong house . . ." she said, trailing off as she glimpsed Ben standing next to me. "Why didn't you tell me you were bringing some-one?" she hissed. "This is really awkward."

"Says the girl who put a guy under her sister's tree. The only thing missing was the bow. You must think I'm completely hopeless."

"Abbie," she started.

"And you were so obvious!" I continued.

"Abbie—"

"I can't believe I didn't see this coming, the way you practically begged me to write that letter to Santa . . ."

"ABBIE!"

"What do you have to say for yourself?!"

"Could you excuse us for a minute?" Grace said sweetly, tossing a smile in Ben's general direction. She grabbed my arm and dragged me, crutches and all, through the doorway and a few steps away, still close enough for Ben to hear. "I have *never* seen that man before in my *life*," she said, slowly yet forcefully.

"Why should I believe you?"

She pointed toward the kitchen. "Because *that's* the guy I got you."

My eyes went immediately to the kitchen table, where a man wearing a nice sweater was sitting. He gave me a slightly crooked half smile, followed by a small wave. I tentatively waved back before turning my face away. I wished that I could just hit pause and give myself a chance to breathe and figure out a plan. I finally looked at Grace, who was staring back at me with wide eyes.

"Are you actually saying that you found *him* under your tree?" she squeaked.

"I thought it was you for sure. If it wasn't you . . ."

She cocked her head, as if seeing me for the first time. "Why are you walking with crutches?"

"Oh, it's such a long story," I said, expelling a breath that somehow dissolved into giggles. Grace started laughing too, and before we knew it, we were both doubled over, trying to catch our breath.

"I hope your guy came with a receipt," I whispered, tears rolling down my cheeks. "I'm going to have a hard enough time returning mine as it is."

"Stop!" Grace said, gasping. "I'm going to wet my pants!"

We finally managed to get ourselves under control and back to the door where Jack and Ben were having a discussion, inexplicably, about lawnmowers.

"So . . . I guess I should just send Chris home," Jack said.

"Don't be silly. We're adults. It's Christmas, and we're all going to have a nice dinner together," she said, the threat in her voice directed at each of us in turn. I never remember her doing that before she had kids—it must be a mom thing.

"Sisters," Jack said, shaking his head. "It's weird. One minute they're pulling each other's hair out, and the next, all is forgiven." Ben smiled at him, and I suddenly had a flash of them watching football together while Grace and I went to the spa.

"Abbie?" Grace said, interrupting my impromptu vision.

"Yes?"

"Are you going to introduce me to your—"

"present?" Jack interrupted, smirking.

"Jack!" Grace said.

"Well, it's what we were all thinking, isn't it?"

"Probably, only no one but you would be tactless enough to say it," she said, giving him a look that said he was going to catch it later.

My present put out his hand and gave Grace his most charming smile. "I'm Ben."

"I'm Grace, and this is my husband, Jack. It's very nice to meet you. I hope you're hungry."

"I'm famished. Your sister hasn't fed me since breakfast, and that was a sparse affair, let me tell you."

"It's not my fault you didn't take advantage of the vending machine at the hospital," I said, hobbling toward the kitchen. Chris was still sitting at the table, but with a decidedly puzzled look clouding his face.

"Why don't I make the introductions?" Grace said, pasting on a smile. "Chris, this is Abbie . . . and her friend, Ben."

As we all shook hands, I thought that only Grace could retain her composure while her matchmaking efforts burned to the ground around her. She rose like a phoenix from the smoldering ashes, ever the perfect hostess. Jack brought another chair and squeezed Ben in next to me.

Morgan gave a brief but sincere prayer.

"Let's eat," Grace said, passing the basket of rolls to Jack.

"Cool crutches!" Jake said.

Hannah tugged on her mother's sleeve, whispering loudly in her ear. "Mom, why did we get Aunt Abbie a man if she was going to bring her own?"

"We'll talk about it later, sweetie."

✳ ✳✳ ✳ ✳✳ ✳

Chris made an early exit, almost before the last bite of pie had been swallowed. I felt really bad about the whole thing, but I certainly didn't plan it that way. While Grace and I did the dishes, the kids forced Ben into the living room, eager to play the new card game I gave them for Christmas. Jack sat on a barstool at the counter, staring off into space with an expression that was, for him, almost thoughtful.

"It wouldn't hurt you to help with the dishes, you know," Grace said, flicking some soapy water in his general direction.

"Women's work," he mumbled quietly.

"What was that?" she demanded.

"You do it so much better than I do, honey."

"That's what I thought you said." Grace handed me a dish, and I rinsed it in the hot water before stacking it in the dish rack. "So," she whispered, leaning closer to me. "How's it going with B-E-N?"

"That's really insulting. Just because I'm dishwashing impaired doesn't mean I can't spell," Jack said.

"That's probably not even his real name." I filled them in on my morning; how when I woke Ben up, he didn't know who he was or where he came from.

"And he let you name him? That's so cute. What if Santa really did bring him?"

"What a bunch of girls!" Jack jeered. "Everyone knows that there is no—"

"Stop right there! Your children are in the next room, so you might want to phrase your next words very carefully."

"I was going to say, there is no . . . way Ben would fit down your chimney."

"Hey, if Santa can fit, there should be ample room for Ben."

"Where is he going to stay?" Grace said, raising her eyebrows.

"We got him a hotel room earlier, before the tragic sledding incident."

Jack snorted. "I can just picture you, flying off the sled—"

"Not. Another. Word," I said.

"Well, I think you should keep him," Jack said.

I looked at Grace and we both got the giggles again.

"What?"

"He's not a stray animal, Jack," I said quietly, hoping that Ben couldn't hear us in the other room.

"I'm serious. Look at him."

I hesitated.

"Go on," he urged.

I peeked into the other room, sneaking a glimpse of Ben. Hannah kept trying to see his cards, and he was carefully guarding them against her prying eyes. Jake said something I couldn't quite catch, and Ben threw his head back and laughed. He looked completely relaxed.

"Well, what do you see?"

"I can see that Hannah cheats at cards, for one thing."

Jack sighed. "He's obviously doing quite well for himself; even his pajamas scream wealth. And, more importantly, he's all alone. Finders keepers, right?"

"Possession is nine tenths of the law?" I said dryly.

"Exactly," Jack said, folding his arms across his chest.

"Sometimes I wonder about you," Grace said.

"The way I see it, Abbie has been looking for someone, and

she wakes up to find this guy asleep under the tree. Problem solved. You're obviously perfect for each other."

"What could possibly lead you to that conclusion?" I asked.

Jack pointed to Ben, who was unwrapping a caramel from the dish resting on the card table. He popped it into his mouth, intentionally chewing it noisily as Morgan blushed.

"You like to make candy. He likes to eat candy."

"A match made in heaven," I said.

"Let me finish—"

"These are really good caramels, Grace," Ben said loudly around a mouthful. The kids laughed harder.

"Why, thank you, but I can't take credit for them. *Abbie* made them," she said, giving me a triumphant look while shaking my arm excitedly with her wet hands.

"I should have known," Ben said.

"So, we both love caramel—big deal. You like my caramels too, but I don't see us forming a rewarding relationship," I whispered to Jack.

"And he likes kids," he said defensively.

"He probably feels at home with your kids because he has a whole house full of them somewhere, along with a beautiful wife who's very worried about him."

"Well, I wouldn't give him up too easily."

"What do you mean?"

"There are a lot of women out there who might try to take advantage of an opportunity like this. You'd better make sure that he really belongs to whoever comes forward to claim him before you just hand him over. If anyone is going to get him, it should be you. You found him," Jack said.

"I think its sweet how you're looking out for Abbie," Grace said, straightening her husband's collar affectionately.

"Someone has to."

I walked over to the card table where Muffy, the family cat, had taken up residence on Ben's lap, begging to be petted. Muffy was a ten-year-old gray Persian who demanded that she be treated with the respect her advanced years deserved. She was also a shameless flirt where men were concerned. Ben patted her lightly, and she looked annoyed until he started scratching behind her ears. Then she purred contentedly.

"I think we'd better get going. I have to get up early, and it's probably past your bedtime as well," I said.

Ben nudged the cat from his lap, sneezing three times in rapid succession. His eyes were suddenly red and watery.

"I guess we know why you're not a cat person."

He sneezed again.

✳ ✳ ✳ ✴ ✳ ✳ ✳

When we got to the car, Ben was still holding the keys, and I reached for them.

"You can't drive."

"Of course I can. Luckily I hurt my left foot, and I only need my right foot to push the pedals." I grabbed for the keys, and he held them above his head, out of my grasp.

"I don't think that's a great idea."

"Yeah, well, that's what I said when you wanted to go sledding, but we still went." I made a little jump, trying to catch him unaware, but succeeded only in a wobbly landing, nearly ending up sprawled on the ground. "Give me the keys!" I said angrily.

"There's no reason for you to drive. I can take you home."

"And how will you get back to the hotel?"

"It's not that far. I can walk."

"It's too cold. I don't want to see on the news tomorrow how they found a guy in his bathrobe, frozen like a popsicle in a snowdrift. Besides, wouldn't you rather that I experimented with driving while someone was around? I'm going to have to drive to work in the morning, so I might as well figure it out tonight when there aren't any people on the roads."

"I'll take you to work in the morning."

"I'm not going to have you chauffeuring me around like I'm an invalid."

"Why not? It's not like I've really got any place to be right now."

"Exactly. You might never have another opportunity to be irresponsible like this. You should sleep late and watch TV and not even bother getting dressed."

"Nah, I'd be bored. Besides, if I don't get out of the bed eventually, the maid won't be able to clean up after me."

"Ah, the truth comes out. Now, its cold, and I want the keys."

He handed them to me, walking around to the passenger side. "I just want to go on record as saying I offered to drive."

I eased myself into the seat. "I'll have the secretary add it to the minutes."

✳ ✳ ✳ ✴ ✳ ✳ ✳

Despite Ben's doubts about my driving abilities, I managed to get us to the hotel quite smoothly. "See? I told you. I'm just fine," I said, unable to resist gloating a little.

"I didn't say you *couldn't* drive. I just said there wasn't any reason that you should."

I considered arguing the point with him, but decided it wasn't worth it.

Ben got out of the car and leaned down, peeking through the open door. "So, will I see you tomorrow?"

"I'll be at the bakery, but you're welcome to come by and I'll put you to work. You might want to buy some clothes first, though."

"Trust me; it's at the top of my to-do list. Are you positive you're okay to drive by yourself?"

"I'm fine. You must be tired. Don't stay up all night watching TV."

"Yes, mother. I'll wait until I wake up some time tomorrow afternoon to turn the TV on."

I shook my head. "Good night."

But he didn't move. He kept his place, his eyes searching mine in silence until I finally had to look away. I felt as if, in those fifteen seconds that felt like fifty, it was too late to retreat someplace safer. He'd seen too much already.

Snowflakes had begun fluttering down, and Ben lifted his eyes to the sky, watching them momentarily. "Have you ever heard that saying about how when you save someone's life, you become responsible for them?"

I was taken aback. The moment had suddenly become too serious, and I felt unprepared, so I tried to lighten the mood. "Yes, but I hardly think that applies to this situation. You can't count carrying me up the hill as saving my life when you were the one who endangered it in the first place."

"That's not what I meant. I think you might have saved mine. Good night, Abbie."

"Good night," I whispered, having a hard time finding my voice.

I couldn't think why, but when Ben closed the door and went inside, it seemed to get colder in the car, as if he'd taken all the warmth with him.

I drove home in a daze, trying to decide whether I felt flattered or just uneasy, all the while telling myself that nothing good could come of letting myself get attached to someone who may or may not already belong to someone else.

It took forever to get myself undressed and into bed with my sprained foot. I hated to think how early I was going to have to wake up to get ready for work on time. I mean, I did own the bakery, and it's not as if there would be someone there wagging their finger at me if I was late, but I still felt a sort of responsibility to the customers. Until now, I hadn't really thought about how difficult it was going to be to cook while I was hopping around the kitchen on one foot.

I took a pain pill and got into bed, flipping on the television for company until I got sleepy. I clicked idly through the channels until I got to the local news. The weatherman informed me that we were in for a few days of sunshine before the next big storm rolled in. It would be nice to get a break from the snow and I thought that maybe I could even go for a long walk in the sunshine, but a sudden sharp pain in my foot reminded me that it probably wasn't the best idea. I'm not sure if it was the pill I took or just the erratic day I'd had, but my eyes were getting heavy. Just as I was about to turn the news off, the next headline caught my attention.

"Now, here's an unusual Christmas story for our viewers out there. A local woman was more than a little surprised at one of the presents she found under her tree." The picture of Ben that was taken at the police station appeared on the screen. I studied it, deciding that it wasn't a bad picture, even if it failed to capture the warm brown of his eyes. "John Doe was asleep in her living room with no memory of how he got there or who he is," the newscaster continued. "If you happen to recognize this man, please call the police station with any information."

"He's pretty good looking," the female newscaster commented. "I wouldn't mind finding him under my tree."

"Well, if no one comes forward to claim him and the lady who found him doesn't keep him, we'll send him to your house," he quipped.

She tittered politely. "That's all we have tonight—"

I flipped off the TV, hoping that Ben hadn't seen it. The commentary made him sound like a piece of meat, for sale to the highest bidder. While I was thinking about calling the station to complain about their insensitivity, I fell asleep.

Seven

* * * * * * * *

I woke up the next morning to my alarm screeching. I gave it a good smack and rolled over onto my side, trying to recall the dream I'd been having. I couldn't remember the whole thing, but towards the end, I was walking through a beautiful green park in springtime, and there was a grove of trees covered in brown seed pods. Upon closer inspection, the seed pods turned out to be slices of bacon, and I started pulling them off the trees and eating them ravenously.

I opened my eyes again suddenly, sniffing the air. It must have been an incredibly vivid dream, because I could almost smell the bacon. In fact, unless I was having some sort of weird painkiller induced hallucination, I swear I could even hear it sizzling in the pan.

I got out of bed gingerly, putting the tiniest bit of pressure on my foot.

"Ow!"

I hopped to where my crutches were resting against a chair, and used them to hobble down the hall. I peered around the corner into the kitchen. Ben stood over a skillet, completely focused on the contents. I was sort of glad to see him, but part of me just wanted to go back to bed and hide, hoping he'd be gone when I ventured out again.

"How did you get in here?" I asked.

"Good morning to you, too. Your door was unlocked."

"No, this time I'm absolutely certain that I locked it behind me when I got home."

"Now if we can just get you to start locking the *back* door, you'll be set. Unless subconsciously, you want me to get in . . ."

I leaned against the doorframe. "What happened to sleeping in and catching up on all your favorite shows?"

"It was tempting, but I thought I'd make you breakfast instead."

"I thought I could smell something."

"Hope you like bacon and eggs," he said, sliding the plate across the table.

"I know that didn't come from my fridge, unless the Breakfast Fairy came last night while I was asleep. And how did you get here?"

"Where are your forks?"

I made my way to the drawer to grab some silverware.

"You sit down," he said. "I'll get it."

"You made breakfast; the least I can do is get the forks," I said dryly. "And you didn't answer my question."

"Public transportation. Did you know there's a bus stop a block from your house? So, I'm providing you with bacon and eggs and saving the environment at the same time."

"Fascinating." I forked a bite of scrambled eggs, which were actually really good.

"Well?" he asked.

"Not bad," I admitted.

He feigned relief. "Good. I was afraid you might be going through cereal withdrawal."

I laughed. "I just don't have time for anything else in the morning."

"Juice?" he asked, pulling a carton from my fridge as if by magic.

✳ ✳ ✳ ✳ ✳ ✳ ✳

"Thank you, that was delicious," I said, swallowing the last of the orange juice.

"I'm glad you liked it."

"I notice your wardrobe is still rather . . . limited."

"The only thing open this early is the 24-hour grocery store."

"Don't forget my all-night bakery."

"You don't sell clothes there, do you?"

"I've been known to put pants on the gingerbread men."

"I think I'll wait for something a little more substantial than icing. Can I drive you to work?"

"I can get there just fine on my own, and in case you haven't noticed, I'm not exactly ready to go."

He waved his hand casually. "You take your time. The stores won't be open for hours."

"Really, don't worry about me. You know what you should do today?"

"Start looking for someone else to pester?"

"No. You should ride the bus around town and see if anything looks familiar. Something might spark a memory."

"Ah, the little tour down No Memory Lane. It would be a lot more fun if you went with me."

"I'm sorry. I wish I could, but I can't. I have to get to work. I'm going to be late already as it is." I put our dishes in the sink, heading toward my room.

"Need any help getting dressed?" Ben's voice trailed after me. Even though I couldn't see him, I could tell from his voice that he was enjoying this.

"I'm locking the door behind me," I called back.

"Don't worry—I'm leaving."

✳ ✳ ✳ ✳ ✳ ✳ ✳

By the time I finally got ready, it was 6:30. I hurried to the car as fast as I could under the circumstances, managing to wedge my crutches into the back before falling into the driver's seat. My foot was already throbbing, and it occurred to me that when I was crossing things off my mental list this morning, I could probably live without the thirty seconds I shaved off by not taking a pain pill. I sifted through my purse, not finding them. They were probably still in my bedroom on the nightstand. The idea of retrieving the crutches, hoisting myself out of the seat, and making my way back to the house seemed too exhausting to contemplate. I'd be fine without the pills until tonight; once I got busy working, I wouldn't have time to notice if my foot hurt or not, right?

Since I was running behind, it was a little closer to being light outside than I was used to. Sometimes I don't like getting up this early, but there's something nice about being one of the only cars on the road and seeing the world before anyone else is awake. Everything is still quiet and unspoiled.

I started backing down my driveway when I noticed my neighbor, Nadine, dart out of her front door, waving. She picked her way through the snow and ice, motioning for me to wait. I sighed. At the rate it was taking her to get to my car, I would be lucky to get to the bakery in time to unlock the door, much less bake anything. And what was she doing up at this hour, anyway? Heaven knows if I didn't have to be up to open the store I'd still be fast asleep in my warm bed. I rolled down my window, and put on a smile.

"Hello, Nadine. What are you doing out so early?"

"I wanted to talk to you, but you keep such strange hours that I've been having a hard time catching you." Nadine was wearing a ratty old housecoat speckled with lint fuzzies and decorated in some of the loudest colors I'd ever seen. In fact, I was glad that the sun wasn't up yet; I was afraid that the house-coat reflecting off the bright white of the snow might have done permanent damage to my eyes. As it was, I could barely look at it in the half light.

"Is there something I can help you with?" I asked, digging into the depths of my soul and forcing as much kindness as I could muster.

"It certainly is cold out here. Why, I bet it's below freezing," she remarked, rubbing her wrinkled hands together before cupping them over her mouth and blowing on them. I could see her little chicken legs sticking out from beneath her housecoat, blue with spider veins and covered with goose bumps until they disappeared mercifully into her furry slippers. "It sure would be nice to warm up in your car while we talk."

I repeated my Nadine mantra in my head: she's old, she's alone, be nice. "Get in, but I only have a few minutes before I have to get to the bakery."

"Well, I'll be as quick as I can, but this is a delicate subject." She crowded her hands near the heating vents, soaking up all the warmth like a sponge and sighing with contentment. "In fact, I was so shocked that I'm not even sure where to begin . . ."

Suddenly it was like a light went on in my head. Nosy Nadine—I knew exactly what she wanted to talk about. As hard as I tried, my mantra went right out the window. "This is about Ben, isn't it?" I demanded.

Nadine looked momentarily disappointed that I'd simply come to the point instead of allowing her to drag out the suspense, but she quickly recovered her composure. "If Ben is the man who you so brazenly strolled out of your house with on Christmas morning, then yes, it is about him."

"That was him."

"So, you admit it!"

"Admit what?"

"That a strange man spent the night at your house. What is the world coming to? I thought you were a good girl!"

"It's not what you think—" I said tightly.

She brushed my argument away with a wrinkled hand, and I could tell she was enjoying this. "That's what they all say."

"No, really, nothing happened."

"Then what was he doing there . . . in his bathrobe? It looks awfully suspicious." She clicked her tongue in a judgmental way, like she was my mother.

"Okay, I know this sounds a little unbelievable, but Santa Claus left him. Ben was my Christmas present."

"Your Christmas present," she repeated slowly.

I told Nadine about how my sister convinced me to ask Santa for a man, since Grace had given up any hope of me finding someone without help. As I gave Nadine the scoop, she listened impassively, without interruption, until I finished. Finally, she spoke. "So, this stranger was just asleep under your tree?"

"Yup."

"In his bathrobe?"

I nodded. "Yeah, that's the whole story. I know it must sound funny, but that's exactly what happened."

Nadine sat silently for a minute, chewing on her fingernail and thinking. She finally turned to me, shaking her head. "I don't know what's worse—that you're a loose woman, or that you lied about it!"

"Nadine! I'm telling the truth! He was even on the news."

"More lies!"

"You watch the news and see. He has amnesia and he can't remember how he got into my house. They're running his picture because they hope someone will recognize him and come forward."

"If I was robbing a house and someone caught me, I'd pretend to have amnesia too."

"It's not like that. He's a really nice guy."

"Whether he's a nice guy or not, he shouldn't be staying in your house. It's not proper."

"He's not staying in my house. He's staying in a hotel room."

That seemed to pacify her a little. "And you like him?"

"He seems okay. It doesn't really matter because as soon as he figures out who he is, he'll be gone."

"Well, I guess I should probably meet him, just in case; see if he's good enough for you."

That was vintage Nadine: one minute she's accusing me of being a floozy, and the next, she's being all protective, wanting to screen my dates.

"I'll bring him around some time and you can tell me what you think."

"I guess that will have to do," she said grudgingly. "I don't suppose you've baked any of those jam tarts I like lately."

"I'll put them on the list."

She sighed. "Well, you're not going to get any baking done sitting around, jabbering at me. The sun's almost up; you're going to be terribly late." She got out of the car and started the precarious journey back to her front door.

I could never decide whether I wanted to hug Nadine or strangle her. So I just backed the car out and drove to work instead.

✴ ✳ ✴ ✴ ✳ ✴

I baked the simplest recipes I could think of that day, and it was still a great deal more difficult than I had expected. I made my rounds through the kitchen on my crutches, gathering ingredients and putting them on the counter. I pulled up a stool so I could sit while I measured and mixed. I made snickerdoodles, and banana bread, and brownies with peppermint frosting. I also made peanut butter cupcakes with a jelly surprise in the middle, not because I was sad, but because they were easy.

Even so, everything seemed to take me twice as long as it normally did, and it was incredibly frustrating. Everybody was really sweet and sympathetic, but after a few rounds of making the trek from the kitchen to help customers, my foot was telling me in no uncertain terms that maybe this wasn't my best plan ever. I found some Tylenol in the cupboard and I gulped a couple down. They helped to make me at least semi-functional, but when I accidentally banged my sprained foot into the door, the agony came back tenfold, and I found myself questioning for the fifteenth time why I hadn't just gone back into the house to get the stupid pain pills.

The lobby was empty, so I hobbled out and carefully lowered myself into one of the chairs. I put my head down on the table, trying to banish the tears in the corners of my eyes that wanted to fall. I knew that once I started crying, it wouldn't be so easy to stop, and that someone could come in any minute. I was glad that it had been slow this afternoon so that no one was there to witness this moment of weakness.

As if on cue, I heard the bell on my door ring, announcing an arrival. I quickly lifted my head up, putting on my bravest smile. Ben came through the door wearing a soft brown leather jacket over a cream colored shirt with jeans and sneakers. The clothes fit him just right, and the sneakers were stiff with shiny newness. I'm not sure whether it was the pain I was in or maybe just seeing him in real clothes, but he looked pretty good to me. I was surprised how glad I was to see him.

"Hey, look who finally got dressed," I said, hoping I sounded more cheerful than I felt.

"Abbie, what's wrong?" he asked, his voice bordering on panic.

"I'm just taking a little break. Everyone must be busy returning Christmas presents because I haven't had very many customers today."

He sat down on the chair next to me. He even smelled good. "You look terrible."

"Thanks a lot."

"You know what I mean. Is your foot worse?"

"No, it's just sore. It's my own fault. I forgot my pills this morning, and I was already late, so I didn't go back for them."

"Abbie . . ." he said disapprovingly, like I was a child who'd been caught doing something naughty.

"I know, I know. It was stupid. You don't have to lecture me."

"I just feel bad. I could have brought them by if I had known."

"Well, you see, I managed just fine."

"But you didn't have to suffer. Speaking of which, I got you something today while I was out." He handed me one of the bags he was carrying and I peeked inside, puzzled at the contents. When I pulled it out, I could see that it was a bright orange throw pillow with a huge smiley face on the front of it.

"A pillow?"

"Isn't it great?"

"Um, yeah, but what am I supposed to do with it?"

He took the pillow from me, put it in the chair across from me, and carefully lifted my foot to rest it on the pillow.

I smiled at him. "I get it now. That was very sweet. Thank you."

"Are you about ready to close up?"

"Almost. Only about an hour left now."

"Would it really be so awful if you closed early?"

"I'm okay. I can hang in there for another hour. Are you hungry?"

"Very. Shopping is hard work."

"Ha ha. Help yourself to anything in the case."

Ben wandered over to the counter, surveying his options. "Everything looks good. It's an impossible choice."

"Have one of everything then."

"I might just do that."

I craned my head around to look at him. "You couldn't eat one of everything."

"Sure I could."

"You'll spoil your dinner," I warned.

"This is my dinner."

"I bet you five dollars you can't do it."

"You're on." He took a tray and started loading it up with assorted goodies from the case. "You know, even if you win, which you won't, you're still going to lose money on the deal."

"I don't care about the money. It will be worth the risk just to prove you wrong."

"Don't be too sure. Can I get you anything?"

"It's okay. I'll just eat what you can't finish."

"Well, you can't say I didn't offer. You're going to be really hungry when the only thing left is crumbs."

"We'll see." He sat down at the table with his overfilled tray. Besides the things I baked that morning, there were also some hazelnut biscotti, chocolate mousse cake, and black and white cookies left over from Christmas Eve. I was fairly confident that there was no way he could plow through it all.

"Where to begin . . ." he said, eagerly scanning the choices. "This looks interesting." He picked up the cupcake, peeling off the paper liner and taking a big bite. He chewed thoughtfully for a minute. "Mmmm . . . peanut butter and jelly. This reminds me of being a kid."

I perked up. "Do you remember anything important, like maybe where you went to school?"

"I remember I had a sack lunch almost every day."

"That's not incredibly helpful."

"Those are really good. I might have to have another one."

On impulse, I took the napkin from his tray, using it to dab a bit of grape jelly from the corner of his mouth. "Maybe you'd better focus on what's in front of you first."

Ben grinned, picking up the thick slice of banana bread. "This tray will be empty before you know it, and I'll be walking out of here with your five bucks in my pocket." He proceeded to demolish the banana bread and the snickerdoodle, but I still had a secret weapon; the chocolate mousse cake. Almost no one makes it through an entire slice of this cake.

Even women who are die-hard chocoholics have admitted defeat. It's just too rich to eat in one sitting.

"Are you getting worried yet?" He was halfway through the peppermint brownie and still showed no signs of slowing.

"Although you have consumed an alarming amount of dessert, you're not quite finished."

After the biscotti and the black and white cookie, there was nothing left on the tray but the chocolate mousse cake. Ben forked a bite confidently and paused with the fork hovering near his lips. "This is going to be a piece of cake."

"Oh, you're so clever."

He chewed the first bite easily, but the second and third bites didn't go down quite so smoothly. He took a deep breath, as if all that pastry was suddenly cutting off his air supply.

"How do you like the cake?" I asked innocently.

"It's very rich," he said, choking on his words.

The slice of cake was massive, and judging from his present difficulties, there was no way he would be able to finish it. I could almost smell the victory.

"Do you have any milk?" he asked.

Before I could answer him, my cell phone rang. I groaned, realizing that I'd left it behind the counter.

"You want me to get it?" Ben said.

"I wouldn't complain. Besides, the cake will still be here when you get back."

He jumped up, grabbing my phone just before I knew it was about to stop ringing. "Abbie's phone," he said. "Yes, this is him. Yes? I understand. I'll be there shortly. Thank you."

By the time he hung up the phone, my curiosity was piqued. "I guess it's a good thing you answered it, since it was for you anyway. Who was it?"

He smiled briefly, but it vanished as soon as it appeared. I wondered if it was the call or just the multiple desserts that made him look a little queasy. "It was the police station. They said they have someone there claiming to be my wife."

Eight

⁜ ✳ ⁜ ✳ ✳ ☀ ✳ ✳ ✳ ✶ ✳ ⁜

"Your wife?" I repeated numbly.

He shrugged. "That's what they said."

"That's such great news," I said, forcing a note of bright-ness into my voice. "I'm so happy for you." If it was such great news, then why was I suddenly feeling like the one who had eaten too many pastries? My stomach was doing flip flops.

"Would you come with me? To the station?"

I hesitated. This was going to be harder than I thought.

"I'm sorry," he amended. "You're in pain. I'm sure you want to get home."

"Of course I'll go with you, if you want me to."

"I know it's silly, but I'm really nervous."

"Don't worry about it. I'm sure that when you see her, everything will come rushing back." Although I felt a little blindsided, it was nothing compared to what Ben must be going through, and I made up my mind that I was going to be strong enough for both of us. "Just let me get my coat and lock up, and we'll be on our way."

I hopped to the coat rack, hardly even noticing the ache in my foot that had been tormenting me all afternoon.

"Let me get that for you," Ben said, helping me into my coat. He stayed behind me and for a minute, neither of us moved. It was as if we were taking stock of this moment together, each knowing that it could be our last. He was so close that I could feel the warmth of his breath on my neck, and no matter how much I wanted to just lean back and let him support me, I knew it wasn't to be. I fought against the desire to surrender and moved away, grabbing my crutches.

"Let's get going. I'm sure your wife has been worried sick, and we don't want to make her wait any longer."

"Abbie . . ."

"Yes?"

"Just so you know . . ."

I looked into his face and saw him struggling for words. As much as I knew what I wanted to hear him say, I prayed that he wouldn't. It would be nice to have something to hold onto later—a souvenir from this brief interlude we'd shared. But at the same time, I didn't want to know.

It turns out I didn't have to worry. The seriousness of his countenance changed to resignation, and the words died on his lips.

"Just so you know," he began again, "I would have finished that cake."

I smiled, wondering how he knew exactly the right thing to say at this uncomfortable moment. "Please. You were two bites away from slipping into a diabetic coma."

He held the door for me as an icy blast of air reminded me that outside, it was still winter. "We'll never know now, will we?"

✳ ✳ ✳ ✳ ✳ ✳ ✳

"If you'll just wait here, sir, I'll bring her in," the officer said, leaving us in a small room with two-way windows.

I balanced my crutches against the wall, taking a seat in one of the chairs. Ben took the chair next to mine but said nothing. It was so silent in the room that I could hear the ticking from the clock on the wall, the second hand ominously counting down the seconds until . . .

Until what? Until Ben remembered who he was and went home to his family? I stole a glance at him, and he too seemed to be mesmerized by the noisy clock. For a man who was about to get his life back, he didn't seem very pleased about it. I heard the muffled sounds of a woman laughing outside, and I wondered if it was *her*. Then again, this wasn't really a laughing moment, unless she was hysterical with joy. If Ben recognized the laugh he didn't show it, merely continuing to focus on the monotonous ticking of the second hand, measuring out the seconds that magically turned into minutes.

Ben put his hand on mine, and I jumped.

"Hey, relax," he said, smiling. "You're not the one in the hot seat."

I realized I'd been tapping my fingers on the table compulsively, probably subconsciously trying to drown out the clock. "I know, but I'm still nervous."

He grinned even wider. "Really? Why?"

I rolled my eyes. "I'm nervous for *you*. Try to keep your ego on a leash, okay?"

"You don't have to get upset. It was just a simple question."

I took a deep breath, trying to quiet the voice in my head that had been asking the same question ever since Ben answered my phone. Why was I so on edge? Ben was about to be reunited with his wife; that was a good thing. And I would be just fine because I'd been smart: I knew from the beginning that this would be the outcome, so I hadn't formed any attachments. His leaving wouldn't affect me in the slightest. Everything would go back to the way things were. I'd get a tall tale to tell, and Ben would get to go home. End of story.

"I wonder if she's on the other side of the glass right now, looking at us," Ben said aloud, interrupting my mental pep talk. Almost immediately the door opened, and a striking brunette woman burst into the room.

"Pookie!" she said, her voice containing equal parts of delight and desperation.

I noticed that Ben's hand still rested on mine, and I pulled my hand away guiltily before looking at her to see if she'd caught on. But her eyes were fixed on Ben, as if she hadn't even noticed I was there. Ben remained frozen where he sat, and I wondered if the force of the moment had brought everything back in a paralyzing flash, or if he was just terrified because he couldn't remember her.

It was a strange scene, to say the least. Ben could only stare—still stunned—while she wore a puzzled expression, as if wondering why she and "Pookie" weren't in each other's arms by now. I kept shifting my stare back and forth between Ben and his wife, and the officer just stood there with his mouth slightly open, breathlessly waiting to see what would happen next. It was like driving by the scene of a particularly gruesome car accident—you know that common decency dictates that you should look away, but no matter how hard you try, you just can't seem to keep your eyes on the road.

I knew that I had to do something. At the rate we were going, the four of us might never leave this room again.

"So," I said casually, "your real name is Pookie?"

This seemed to jar Ben enough to bring him around. "Of course my name isn't Pookie." When *she* didn't comment, he frowned. "Seriously, my name isn't Pookie, is it?"

She tossed her hair back as she laughed, looking like a shampoo commercial. "No, I'm the only one who calls you Pookie. Your name is Elliott, silly."

I felt my stomach drop to my toes. This was really happening. Ben's name wasn't really Ben; it was Elliott, and he was really married to *her*.

Ben/Elliott shook his head slowly. "I'm so sorry, but I don't remember you at all."

"My name is Veronica. Veronica Gordon."

"So, I'm Elliott Gordon?"

"No, you're Elliott Sanders," she corrected.

"I thought you were his wife," I said. She finally looked at me, smiling gratuitously.

"I'm his fiancée, but we're about as close to being married as you can get without actually saying the words. The wedding is in three days." She slid up to Ben's chair, putting her hands blatantly on his shoulders so I couldn't miss the giant rock gleaming on her finger. "I don't think I caught your name," she said, shooting me a pearly smile full of daggers.

"Her name is Abbie," Ben interjected.

"Oh, riiiight. You must be the girl they mentioned on television—the one who found my Elliott."

"That's me," I said, trying to keep the bitterness out of my voice.

"I was afraid you'd gotten cold feet, Pookie, until I saw your face on the news. You must have been sleepwalking."

"Is that something I do?"

"I wouldn't know. I guess once we're sleeping in the same bed, I'll be able to keep a closer eye on you." She giggled as she squeezed Ben, her red fingernails curling into his shoulders like claws in a very visual display of ownership.

"This just doesn't make sense to me. I can't believe that we're getting married because I don't know you at all. I would think that at least a small part of me would recognize you."

"I don't know what happened to your memory, but we just have to give it some time. It will all come back eventually, I promise."

"But you can see why I can't exactly go through with the wedding right away."

"Everything is arranged! The church, the caterer, the cake, not to mention the invitations have been sent. We just have to get married!" She fluttered the lashes on her wide eyes like a cartoon animal.

"I can't marry someone I don't remember," Ben said gently.

"Well, maybe you'll remember this," she said, pulling his face to meet hers. The officer and I both gasped as she pressed her lips against his hungrily. They kissed for what seemed like minutes, and I noticed, with no small amount of irritation, that Ben didn't exactly seem repulsed by the whole thing. She finally had to pull away for air. Ben looked dazed, and there was another emotion on his face as well that I couldn't quite place.

"Well?" she said.

"I really hate to ask you this, and it's not that that wasn't lovely, but don't you have some sort of proof that we're a couple?" Ben asked finally.

"Like what?"

"How about a wedding invitation?"

"We sent them all out."

"What about just something that verifies who I am? Like my driver's license."

"I figured you'd taken it with you. They asked me to bring it to the police station, but I couldn't find it anywhere. Maybe you lost it when you were sleepwalking."

"Birth certificate? Social security card?"

"I don't know where you keep stuff like that."

"There must be something."

"Come with me. I'll take you to dinner and we'll talk, and then we'll go back to your apartment. I'm sure you'll start remembering things like crazy."

Ben hesitated. "I guess it couldn't hurt to have dinner."

Veronica took his hand, pulling him out of the chair. "Excellent. Let's get going. Oh, and Abbie, is it? I wanted to thank you for taking such good care of my Pookie for me."

"It was nothing," I said, careful to keep my voice flat.

"No really, you were great," Ben said.

"You're not so bad yourself," I added, allowing myself a tiny smile.

Ben/Elliott grabbed my crutches and brought them to me.

"Can I help you out to your car?"

"Thanks, but I can take it from here. You, go . . . get your memory back."

Veronica was steering him toward the door, and all I could

do was stand there with my crutches and watch him go. She linked her arm through his and laid her head on his shoulder as they walked away.

"Well, I guess that's that," the officer said. "It's kind of nice to see a happy ending for a change."

"Happy for whom?" I growled under my breath. Suddenly, something in my brain locked into place. I went as fast as I could, burning rubber on my crutches as I hobbled after them. They were almost to the main door of the police station now, and I knew I'd never catch them.

"Ben!" I yelled.

He stopped, turning around to face me. "Yeah?"

"Hang on just a minute." I made my way to where they had stopped. Veronica actually had her hand on the door, and she looked more than a little annoyed.

"I just have one more question for you, Veronica," I said, a little out of breath.

She looked like she was considering strangling me, but by some supreme effort, she managed a civil reply. "Yes?"

"Is Ben, I mean, Elliott, a cat person or a dog person?"

She sighed heavily. "We have three cats that we adopted from the shelter. Pookie insisted that we name them Larry, Moe, and Curly, even though they were all girls. Isn't that funny?"

I grabbed Ben's arm. "Okay, that's it. We're through here."

"Elliott! What's going on? What is she talking about?" she said, her voice getting more shrill with every word.

"*Ben* couldn't possibly be your fiancé because he's incredibly allergic to cats."

"I am, actually," he said sheepishly.

The look on Veronica's face said that she knew she was busted, but that didn't stop her from giving Ben a shameless smile.

The officer, who had rejoined us at some point, glared at the woman. "This isn't a joke, miss. Do you know that this

gentleman could press charges against you for falsely repre-
senting yourself?" I could tell he was trying to sound stern,
but he looked like he was on the verge of falling under her
spell.

Her smile wilted and faded away. "I only wanted to meet
a nice guy. It's so hard to find someone, and he was so . . .
available—"

Ben held up one hand, stopping her speech. "It's all right.
I'm not going to press charges."

She tilted her head toward him. I couldn't believe she was
still flirting with him after everything that had happened.

"Where did you get the ring?" I demanded.

"I borrowed it from a friend."

"How were you going to explain having to give the ring
back? Or the wedding in three days that never materialized?"

"I hadn't really thought that far ahead." She turned her
attention back to Ben. "Maybe you want to go out for a drink
or something? We could start over again, put this behind us. It
would make a great story of how we met."

"I appreciate the offer, and although it is memorable,
this story still isn't as good as finding someone under your
Christmas tree. I think I'm going to have to stick with that
one, for now."

Veronica looked at me jealously, and I looked down at
the brown linoleum, not daring to glance at Ben. She took a
notepad and a pen from her bag, scribbling something down.
"This is my name and number. Give me a call if you change
your mind."

I watched as her long, skinny legs disappeared down the
steps and into the parking lot before I let out a sigh of disgust.
She'd even given the officer an almost timid look as she left, as
if she were some demure damsel in distress. She left with her
head held high, as though she'd done the community some
great service instead of being busted trying to commit fraud.
Ben and the officer were watching her exit with great interest. Once she was out of sight, Ben handed the number to the

officer, and they grinned at each other.

"Thanks, man," the officer said, shaking Ben's hand.

"No problem."

"I don't believe this! You do know she's crazy, right?" I barked.

"Yeah, but she's hot," he said, tucking the note into his pocket.

✳ ✳ ✳ ✴ ✳ ✳ ✳

"Well, that was interesting," Ben said, turning the key in the ignition of my car. He'd offered to drive, and I let him. I was still too angry to think clearly.

"Interesting? How can you say that? It was awful. How could anyone mess with somebody like that?"

"Aw, she was just lonely."

"That's no excuse! She's lucky you're such a nice guy, because if she'd tried to sell me that load of crap, I *would* have pressed charges."

"I don't think you're really her type, so you probably don't have to worry about it."

"You know what I mean. I might be lonely, but I wouldn't use someone who was at a disadvantage just to get into a relationship."

"I, for one, wouldn't complain if you used me," he said, and I smiled wanly. "Are you really lonely?" he asked.

"Sometimes," I admitted.

"Yeah, me too."

"Have you remembered something?"

"I wouldn't call it a memory—more of an impression."

"What do you mean?"

"Well, when I was playing cards with your nephew and nieces, I had this sort of . . . longing feeling. Like I knew I didn't have any kids, and I wished I did."

"Maybe that feeling was just you missing your own kids;

wishing you could be with them."

Ben looked right into my eyes. "I'd like to think that if I had kids, nothing could ever make me forget that."

I struggled to take an even breath. "And your wife? What about her?"

"I suppose it's possible, but I just can't imagine something like that being completely wiped from my memory. No matter what else I forgot, deep down, I would always remember that." His voice was soft but, at the same time, firm and unyielding, and I marveled at his conviction, when so much in his life was uncertain. "So, since I can't tell you my reasons for not being married—"

"—if you aren't—"

"—if I'm not, which I'm pretty sure of, why aren't you married?"

"I told you already. The right guy for me doesn't exist."

"That sounds pretty final. Something really awful must have happened to lead you to that conclusion."

"Not one awful thing; lots of awful things in succession."

"Now we're getting somewhere. Tell me about what it is that's made you so averse to the idea of relationships."

I sighed, trying to organize my thoughts. "You know, I'm the last person I ever would have thought would still be single. I fell in love over and over again, ever since I was old enough to say the word."

"Oh, you were *that* girl," Ben said, chuckling.

"Yeah, I remember coming home from school and telling my mother about the latest boy I'd sworn my undying devotion to. And she'd say, 'Abbie's in love—it must be Wednesday.' "

"So what happened?"

"It wasn't any one thing that happened. It was a series of relationships that came crashing down around me, one after the other. Love is great while it lasts; it's the abrupt thud at the end that I couldn't get used to."

"Maybe you really weren't in love all those times. Maybe you've never really been in love at all," he ventured.

"I don't know. It always felt real at the time."

"Well, I'm probably not the person to be lecturing anyone about relationships, but maybe you're just really unlucky. Maybe you've been in love a lot of times, but you just haven't met the right guy yet. Sometimes, people are born with really big hearts, and it turns out to be a curse instead of a blessing. They fall in love a lot easier than other people and end up getting burned. Love is trial and error, Abbie; you just have to keep trying."

"Trust me—after the horse throws you repeatedly, the ride loses some of its appeal."

Ben laughed, but his reply was serious. "And you're okay with being single?"

"Yes," I said immediately, not pausing to let myself consider the answer.

"But if a hypothetical someone were to show an interest . . ." he pressed.

"Hypothetically, I'm not sure. I guess I would have to see how I felt in the moment. I just got tired of getting hurt, you know?"

He nodded. "Well, this is my stop. Thanks for the ride."

"I know you must be disappointed. I'm sorry it didn't work out," I said.

But I wasn't. I hobbled around to the driver's seat, waved to Ben as he went inside, and wondered about our conversation as I drove home. Part of me wanted to believe that he was the hypothetical someone who could change my mind. But as quickly as the thought entered my brain, I sent it away. I wasn't about to give my heart to someone who, in all probability, belonged to someone else. Just because tonight was a false alarm didn't mean that Ben's real wife might not turn up tomorrow, despite his assurances about knowing he couldn't be married. Ben was too perfect not to have been snapped up by someone already. As far as I was concerned, it was only a matter of time before the real Mrs. SBC stepped forward, and then I would be right back where I started.

Nine

When I opened my eyes in the morning, the first thing I noticed was that my foot didn't hurt quite as much as the day before. I flexed it gently, testing it to see if it was really getting better or if it had just gone numb. I was fairly certain I wasn't ready to go without the boot and the crutches yet, but at least I could move my foot now without setting off a series of painful fireworks in my leg.

I got out of bed and got ready for work, telling myself that I didn't really miss Ben's company at breakfast as I bolted down a quick bowl of Honey Nut Cheerios. Despite strict admonishments to myself to banish him to the far outer reaches of my imagination, I couldn't help wondering what he was doing this morning.

I didn't have to wonder for very long.

As I pulled into the parking lot, I noticed a man in a dark coat, sitting on the little bench next to the door of the bakery. It was hard to tell in the early morning gloom, but he seemed friendly enough as he waved a gloved hand. It could only be one person. What would Ben be doing here at this hour? I dragged myself out of the car and onto my crutches, the sound of my car door slamming echoing like an explosion in the quiet dawn.

"You really do get here at five," Ben said as I approached

the door. His cheeks were pink, and his breath clung to the frosty air.

"I told you I did. Did you really get up this early just to see if I'd be here on time?"

"No, I'm actually here to offer my services. Hurry up and open the door—it's freezing out here!"

"How long have you been waiting?"

"About twenty minutes. I got here a little early, but I wasn't worried because I figured the door would be open. Imagine my surprise to find it locked."

I turned the key in the lock, rushing into the warmth of the bakery. "Of course I wouldn't leave it unlocked. What were you thinking?"

"You never manage to lock the door to your home."

"This is different. The bakery is my livelihood—"

"Whereas at home, only your life is in danger. It's all making perfect sense now," he said, hanging his jacket on the coat rack.

"What did you mean when you said you were here to offer your services?"

"I'm here to help, so you can put me to work. Today I become . . . a baker," he announced.

"But *why* are you here to work?"

"You had such a difficult time yesterday that I thought you might be open to a little assistance."

"I can manage by myself, and I remembered these today, so everything will be fine," I said, shaking the bottle of pain pills.

"Let's just say that I'm working off my debt, then."

"You don't owe me anything."

"Well, for one thing, I owe you for unmasking that impos-ter last night."

"That was pretty spectacular," I admitted.

"Right, let's get going. What do you want me to do?"

"Go wash your hands."

"Yes, ma'am," he said heading for the sink, leaving me to wonder what I was going to do with him all day.

"Okay, hands washed. What's next?"

"Grab an apron," I said, pointing to some hooks on the wall. Ben took the white apron and tied it around his waist. "The white one is my favorite," I complained.

"Abbie, I'm here to help, and with good intentions, but I draw the line at wearing the one with the flowers on it."

"All right," I said grudgingly, slipping on the offending flowered apron. I took one of my recipe books from the shelf and started flipping through it randomly. "Now, let's see . . ." I stopped at one page, setting it open on the counter as I reached for another book. I hobbled to the fridge, pulling open the door and scanning the contents. This went on for about a minute.

"Don't you have some sort of routine?" Ben interrupted.

"What do you mean?"

"You look like you're the one with amnesia. It's like you've never done this before."

"Well, I get here and I look through my recipes and see what ingredients I have, and then I decide what I'm going to make."

"You don't make the same things every day?"

I laughed. "How boring would that be? I wouldn't last two weeks if I had to make the same thing over and over again. I'd go nuts."

"But how do you decide?"

"I make what I feel like making."

"What about your customers? Aren't they disappointed when they come in craving something they had last time, only to find it missing?"

"Some are, but I've had lots of people tell me that they discovered a favorite because they were forced to try something new. Sometimes people like being surprised."

Ben shook his head. "I don't know. If I had to come up with a new menu every morning, I'd never get anything done. I like to get into a routine."

"Maybe you were an accountant," I suggested, a smile curling my lips.

"Very funny. So, what are we making today?"

"What do you like?"

"Everything except pineapple . . . and dark chocolate."

"But that chocolate mousse cake had a dark chocolate ganache."

"Yeah, I know," he said, pulling a face.

"Then why did you eat it?"

"That was different. It was a bet."

"What if I had told you it was chocolate worm cake?"

"A bet is a bet."

I shuddered. "I guess I just don't understand that guy mentality. So what would you make if this was your bakery?"

"I love oatmeal raisin cookies."

"Okay." I started flipping through the cookbook I was holding. "I know I have a good recipe here somewhere . . ."

"No need. I think I've got it covered."

I stopped, thinking he must be joking. "Okay, Amnesia Boy. You go right ahead."

"I'm serious. I don't need a recipe."

"Look, it's not that I don't believe you. It's just, there's a reason there are recipes for cooking. Recipes have rules, and they're very specific. When you don't follow the recipe exactly, things tend to go terribly wrong."

"What happened to people liking surprises? This doesn't sound like the free-wheeling Miss Spontaneity of five minutes ago."

I studied him for a minute, trying to judge from his expression whether he was just playing with me, but his eyes met mine firmly with an unreadable stare that gave nothing away. I walked to the cupboard where I took out the canister of oatmeal. I handed it across the counter to him. "Knock yourself out."

"Could I have a bowl and a spoon?"

I retrieved the items he requested along with various measuring cups, which he refused.

"I don't need to measure it." He began scooping random

spoonfuls of oatmeal into the mixing bowl. Time and again he dipped the spoon, the mound of oatmeal in the bowl growing higher and higher until I couldn't take it any longer.

"What are you doing?"

"Diving for pearls. What does it look like I'm doing? I'm making cookies."

"Really? Because it looks like you're moving the oatmeal from one container to another . . . very slowly."

He laughed as he continued his spooning. "Wait until I get to the part with the flour."

"I'm pretty sure that's not how you do it." I was trying to be patient, but it was no good.

"What you mean is that's not how *you* do it."

"Yes. Me and everyone else out there who knows how to cook."

Ben went to the pantry, scanning the shelves before returning with a bag of raisins. He started throwing handfuls indiscriminately into the bowl with the oatmeal.

"You can't put the raisins in now!" I said, panicking. "The raisins go in last."

"Abbie, what's the worst thing that could happen? If I'm wrong, you're out a couple of bucks in ingredients. But if I'm right, you have a great new recipe."

I harrumphed. "You say that like you think I could dupli-cate this . . . mess."

"I'll write it down for you."

"What? Mix twenty-five spoonfuls of oatmeal with four handfuls of raisins . . ."

"See, you're getting the hang of it already. Now, I bet you have plenty of other work to do, unless my cookies are the only thing on the menu today. Why don't you start baking some-thing else and leave me to my mess?" He put his hands on my shoulders, gently steering me in the direction of the cupboard.

In keeping with the raisin theme, I started to make dough for cinnamon rolls. Every now and then, I stole a curious glance at Ben, watching incredulously as he measured various ingredients in the palm of his hand. Everything I'd ever learned about cooking involved recipes, and Ben was flying in the face of reason. I got the feeling from his slap-dash attitude toward cooking that he would probably be the kind of person who would order pizza with all of the really bizarre toppings on the list that no one ever chooses.

While the dough was rising, I made mini carrot cakes. As I was shredding the carrots, the kitchen began to fill with the enticing smell of toasty spices. I headed nonchalantly in the direction of the oven, only to be shooed away by Ben. "No peeking!"

I gave him a haughty look. "I only came over for the muffin tins."

By the time he took the tray from the oven, my mouth was watering. I followed him like an eager puppy as he removed them to cool on a wire rack. "Would you like to try one?" he asked innocently, holding out the metal spatula with a perfectly browned cookie perched on top.

I took it, examining it from all angles. "Well, it looks okay," I said, sniffing it. I bit into the cookie. It was crispy on the outside and chewy on the inside with a hint of cinnamon. It was everything that an oatmeal raisin cookie should be.

"Well?"

"It's a miracle." I took another bite, just to be sure. "I'm having trouble figuring out how this is possible. These are the best oatmeal raisin cookies I've ever had."

"Don't you feel sorry for making fun of me now?"

"Yes, but I don't understand. Your recipe, or lack of, goes against everything I've ever learned about cooking."

"Sometimes you have to be willing to take chances."

"Not with cooking."

"Maybe I wasn't talking about cooking."

I pretended like I didn't hear him. "These are amazing. What else can you make?"

"That's it. I'm afraid I only know one trick."

"People are going to love them."

"You think?"

"Absolutely."

He beamed, busying himself shaping more dough into balls while I worked on the cinnamon rolls. Meanwhile, the doorbell rang, announcing the first customers of the day.

"I'll go help them. You just keep doing what you're doing," Ben said. I watched him intently from the kitchen as he helped Mrs. Norton choose her breakfast. She came in regularly, at least three times a week on her way to work. She kept looking around the bakery, at first curiously, then desperately, as if she were afraid that Ben had been in the process of robbing me and was forced to assume the identity of a friendly employee when she walked in. Finally, as he was counting out her change, she ventured, "I come in here a lot, and I've never seen you before. Where is Abbie?"

I poked my head around the corner. "I'm right here, Mrs. Norton."

She let out a sigh of relief. "Thank heavens. I was convinced that either I was going to find you tied up in a corner somewhere or I was losing my mind!"

Ben laughed, putting out his hand. "I'm Ben, the new houseboy. I'm working off my debt to Abbie."

She shook his hand. "Nice to meet you, Ben. I'm glad Abbie is finally getting a little help around here—she works too hard." She noticed the row of Ben's oatmeal raisin cookies in the case and pointed to the note card. "What are amnesia cookies?"

"Ben made them," I said, and he puffed up his chest proudly. "He's having a little trouble with his memory right now," I whispered loudly.

Mrs. Norton's eyes widened. "Now that you mention it, I think I saw you on the news!" She looked at us both as if we had suddenly attained celebrity status. "Did you really find him under your Christmas tree?"

"I did. Santa outdid himself this year, don't you think?"

Mrs. Norton nodded appreciatively, and Ben ducked his

head shyly. "Ladies, please, I'm getting embarrassed. How about trying one of these cookies?"

"I don't know. Amnesia cookies sound pretty sketchy."

"I had a hard time believing it myself, but they're excellent," I assured her.

Her eyes narrowed as she surveyed Ben a little more closely. "Do you really have amnesia?"

His face took on a blank expression, and he turned to me suddenly as if I was his keeper and he was only out on a day pass. "I can't remember. Do I?"

I managed to keep a straight face momentarily before bursting into wild laughter. By then, Ben was laughing too, putting his hand on my arm to steady himself. Mrs. Norton just looked at us as if we were both crazy. "I guess I'll try one."

"You won't regret it," Ben promised.

✳ ✳✳ ✳ ✳ ✳ ✳

We took a quick break around lunch, eating the ham sandwiches I made for myself before I left the house. Ben ate heartily, chasing his sandwich with all the cookies he could eat.

"Where are you putting all that food?" I marveled.

"I have hollow legs. Besides, I've worked really hard today."

"It's only lunch time. There's still plenty of work left to do."

He groaned. "How do you do this every day?"

"I love it. I can't imagine doing anything else. But you don't have to stay. I'm not really going to force you to work off your nonexistent debt."

"No, I'm having fun."

"You don't have to say that."

"I really am having a good time."

"Well, if you don't mind keeping an eye out for customers, I'll get a cake in the oven."

"What kind of cake?"

"How about lemon cheesecake with a gingersnap crust?"

"Yes, ma'am," he said, saluting sharply as he went out to supervise the register.

✻ ✻ ✻ ✻ ✻ ✻ ✻

As the afternoon went on, Ben proved himself to be an excellent houseboy. He laughed and joked with the customers, who stared curiously at the good-looking stranger who had unwittingly ensconced himself in the bakery and my life. When he reminded me that it was time to take my pain pill, instead of finding myself annoyed at the intrusion, I was surprised to discover that I was charmed. It was strangely reassuring to have someone around who not only knew about the rhythms of my day, but cared about my comfort. It was also a little bit unnerving.

One of my friends, Iris, stopped by at about 3:00. I met her in the first few weeks I was open when she wandered into the bakery, crying, a stranger looking for a phone book. I was alarmed, thinking that some sort of accident had occurred, and I asked her if there was anything I could do. She said no, not unless I was willing to trade places with her for a week and entertain her vicious mother-in-law. It turned out that Iris's husband had neglected to mention that his mother was coming to stay, calling from work at lunch to ask if she could please pick Mummy up at the airport and have dinner ready by six. He also told her to wear something nice for a change, specifically not the appallingly ugly green shirt she had on when he left for work.

Iris and her husband are divorced now. I don't know exactly what role the episode with her mother-in-law played in the demise of their marriage, but I think it was due more to his habit of verbally belittling her. Nothing she ever did was good enough, and although she's been away from him for almost two years now, her self-esteem still suffers. But she and I have managed to make significant strides over good chats and vast quantities of pastry.

I was watering the plants when she walked in. I don't know why I bother with growing plants; they've never lasted very long. I've tried everything. Once, I watered them too much, and then not enough. I never fertilized, and then I over-fertilized. I tried them in sun and shade; I even tried talking to them. But it was no good. My mother gave me one she said was foolproof, but almost immediately it took a turn for the worse. It was as if something in the air surrounding me was toxic to anything leafy. Every couple of months, I went out and bought more, but it was only a temporary solution. I had now come to accept that my bakery was the place plants went to die.

I waved Iris over. "I haven't seen you in weeks! I'm so glad you came by."

Iris pulled out a chair and sat down, and I took the chair next to her. "Well, I felt like something sweet this afternoon." She glanced across the room, surveying Ben in his white apron. "Looks like you beat me to it."

"He doesn't look half bad behind the counter, does he? Kind of dresses up the place."

"If he's going to be working here, I'm going to be broke and fat because I'll have to come in every day."

My smile faded. "He's not going to be working here much longer, so your wallet and your waistline are safe."

"Did the temp agency send him?" she said.

"Not exactly."

"Then where did you find him?"

"You wouldn't believe me if I told you." I explained my wildly improbable Christmas morning, and Iris listened intently, sneaking a look at Ben every now and then.

"I had no idea that Santa had such good taste. I know exactly what I'm going to ask for next year . . ."

"Oh, please. Obviously something must have happened

to him that wiped his memory, and he just wandered in. You don't really think that Santa just packed him up in the sleigh with all of the other toys, do you?"

"Stranger things have happened."

"Name one."

"I'd have to think about it. But why couldn't it be true? I have an aunt who swears she saw Santa Claus once."

"Now you're just messing with me."

"No, I'm serious! But nobody believed her because she'd just had surgery . . . and it wasn't Christmas."

I rolled my eyes at her, but she continued.

"What does it matter how he got here?" she whispered, pointing at Ben who was now scrubbing at a stubborn spot on the counter with a rag. "He's really hot, has no memory and therefore no heinous mother, and he's *cleaning*. It looks to me like you've got it made."

"Think about it; can you honestly picture him working here? Look at him—he could do anything. He's probably a business executive or a doctor or a—"

"male model?" she interrupted.

Despite my darkening mood, I still managed a wry smile. "He's not going to stick around. The minute he remembers where he came from, he'll be gone, and that's that."

"Oh, Abbie, cheer up. Maybe he'll never get his memory back, and you can keep him."

"You sound just like my brother-in-law."

"Well, why not?"

"Because he's not a lost puppy. Even if he never remembers, that doesn't mean he'll want to stay here." I watched Ben for a minute as he waited patiently while a woman agonized over her choices. It was almost like he could sense me watching, and he suddenly looked in my direction. He glanced briefly at Iris, then back to me, giving me the bashful smile of someone who knows he's being discussed before turning his attention back to the woman who'd finally made her decision.

"Funny, he doesn't look like he's going anywhere," Iris

said, pulling me out of the moment and grounding me once again in the present.

"Haven't you learned by now?" I said quietly. "None of them stay forever, not even the really good ones. The minute you give in and let yourself feel something, they're gone." There was no bitterness in my tone, only resignation.

"That is incredibly depressing."

"It's reality."

Ben's customer was going, and he took advantage of the break in our conversation to approach the table. "I was going to just surprise you girls, but I've learned that one should never presume with women, especially not where dessert is concerned." He turned to Iris. "Can I get you something . . . ?" he trailed off, and I realized he didn't know her name.

"This is my friend, Iris," I said. "Iris, this is Ben."

She shook his hand, and I noticed that her face was considerably pinker. Iris has curly red hair and creamy skin peppered with millions of light freckles, which always looked amazing with that green shirt her ex-husband couldn't stand. But if she gets embarrassed or shy, you can actually see her blush spread. She hates it, but I can see how men would find it adorable.

"It's very nice to meet you, Iris. Can I tempt you with something from the case?"

"I'll have a piece of that chocolate mousse cake I had last time, if you've got any."

"I'm afraid that I ate the last piece myself," Ben admitted. "Can you ever forgive me?"

"Since we just met, I'm going to give you the benefit of the doubt."

"As a token of my sincere apology, anything else you would like is on me."

"That's very sweet, but you don't have to."

"I insist. What can I get you?"

I jumped up. "I know what Iris likes. Why don't the two of you chat while I go pick something?" I suggested, hurrying off in the direction of the kitchen before anyone could protest.

I ducked down behind the case, taking my time getting a plate and choosing something so I could watch them through the glass.

I'd never seen Iris around a guy she was interested in before and whether she knew it or not, she liked him. I could tell. I found myself thinking that Ben was just the kind of man she deserved. I stole a look nonchalantly as they chatted, and I noticed with satisfaction that Iris didn't appear nearly as nervous as she usually was. Ben laughed at something she said, and she fairly glowed with happiness.

"Here you go . . . one mini carrot cake with cream cheese frosting," I said, sliding the plate in front of her. "Can I get you anything?" I asked Ben.

"I'm just fine. What are we doing now?"

"I'm going to go work on a couple of pies. Why don't you keep Iris company for a minute? I'm sure you could use a break."

He looked hesitant for a moment before breaking into an easy grin. "Sure. Why not?"

I went into the kitchen, feeling a bit like I'd just given my best teddy bear to the less fortunate neighbor girl down the street. I knew it was a noble thing I was doing, but it still stung. I started peeling apples for pie, chewing some of the crunchy, tart skins thoughtfully. After pushing away my initial feelings of regret, I comforted myself with the idea that Iris needed a Ben much more than I did.

✳ ✳✳ ✳ ✳✳ ✳

Ben came into the kitchen just when I was setting the timer on the oven. He went straight to the sink and started washing the dirty bowls. I picked up a towel and waited for him to rinse them in the hot water. As he passed the bowl to me he looked into my face, but we still didn't speak. We washed all of the dishes in silence, and I killed a few seconds by going to the oven and peering through the door to check on the progress of the pies. They looked the same as they had when I put them in there five minutes ago.

Something was wrong. I turned around to face Ben, an artificial smile on my face, as he finally spoke.

"Why were you trying to pawn me off on your friend?" he said quietly.

"What's wrong with Iris?"

"There's nothing wrong with her. She seems like a great girl."

"She is, and she's smart, and sweet, and she hasn't had an easy life. You would be perfect for her."

"Why?"

"Because you're such a nice guy."

"I'm glad you think so, but I don't think Iris and I are right for each other."

"Why not?"

He paused for a minute. "Well, what about that wife you keep warning me about; the one who might be out there somewhere looking for me?"

"You mean the one you said doesn't exist?"

"Yes, but you could be right. Would you want your friend to get hurt?"

"No!"

"Then what was all that about? Leaving us out there to get acquainted was about as subtle as a wrecking ball."

"I thought you might be interested. Iris was."

"Did she tell you that?"

"She didn't have to—I could tell. She was blushing all over the place."

"Well, that just goes to show how much you know about matchmaking. She talked about you the entire time; what a good friend you were when she didn't have anybody and how selfless and caring you are. While you were in the kitchen leaving us alone, she was working her little heart out pleading your case."

I sighed, trying to pretend I wasn't relieved. As far as I was concerned, Iris was getting free dessert for life. "I just thought you two might make a good couple."

"I think it might be too late for that."

As much as I didn't want to look at him, I couldn't help it. In fact, it was almost as if I had no choice in the matter. Whether it was fate, or the way the stars and planets were aligned, or maybe just two people being in the right place at the right time, I couldn't fight the way my eyes were drawn to his at that moment any more than I could magically change the current season from winter to spring. His eyes burned with an intensity that startled me, and I realized that the impatient humming in my ears was the increasingly rapid beating of my own heart. I remember thinking, *This is it. This is the one thing that has been missing from my life, this feeling of reckless anticipation.* I knew that I should push this away, push him away, for many different reasons, but mostly because I knew that once I surrendered myself to this impulse, going back to regular, everyday life would be like stepping into a black and white photograph. It was one thing to live in that photograph, not knowing what touching colors felt like. But once I'd dabbled in the brightness of blues and reds and greens, going back to my monochromatic existence would be unbearable.

All this and infinitely more raced through my mind in the five seconds before I calmly replied, "Really? Why?"

"Because I think I'm falling for someone else."

My cell phone rang.

I closed my eyes briefly in frustration. It was like someone had pulled the plug on a plastic blow-up beach ball, and all the tension in the room slowly deflated. I gave Ben a quick smile, checking my phone to see who it was.

"I'm sorry, it's my parents. I haven't talked to them since before Christmas. My mother is probably wondering if I'm still alive."

"Go ahead. I don't mind," Ben replied.

"Thanks," I said pushing the talk button. "Hello?"

"Abbie? Is that you?" I immediately recognized my mother's worried tone.

"Who else would it be?"

"Well, it's about time. I was beginning to think you'd been kidnapped!"

"I'm just fine."

"If you're just fine, then why haven't you been answering your phone?" she demanded.

"I've been out a lot . . . and I've been working."

"That's why you have a cell phone, isn't it? So your poor mother doesn't have to lie awake, imagining you lying in a ditch somewhere."

I cringed. "It's been lost. I just found it this morning. You know what they say—when something is lost, it's almost always behind the refrigerator," I chirped inanely.

"How did your phone get behind the refrigerator?"

"It wasn't really behind the fridge, Mom. It's just an expression."

"Never mind, did you get the package we sent you?"

"Yes, it was very nice. But why did you send me underwear and socks?" Ben looked amused, and I suddenly wished that I had let the phone ring. I could have called her back later and saved myself the embarrassment.

"I've always given you underwear and socks for Christmas, since you were a little girl."

"I know, but I'm perfectly capable of buying my own . . . stuff now."

"What can I say—old habits die hard. So . . . how was your Christmas? What did Santa bring you?"

"Have you been talking to Grace?" I said, immediately suspicious.

"No. Apparently, her phone has been behind the refrigerator as well. I was going to try her again after I talked to you. Why?"

Now that I knew she didn't know anything, I wished I hadn't brought it up, especially with Ben standing right next to me, smirking. How does one explain to one's mother that Santa brought her something a little unconventional this year? "It's nothing," I said, brushing her off and hoping she would take the hint. Unfortunately, my mother had never been particularly intuitive as far as hint-taking was concerned.

"It must be something because of the way you reacted."

It was unavoidable now. She would be like a dog with a bone until I caved. "Santa brought me a man for Christmas," I mumbled into the phone.

"What? Santa brought you a van?"

"No, a man, Mom. A *man*!" I yelled. Ben was grinning widely now, leaning back against the sink with his arms folded across his chest, waiting to see how this would play out.

"What do you mean, Santa brought you a man?"

"It's a long story, Mom."

"Well, I called you and I'm willing to pay the phone bill. Let's hear it."

"The short version is that I left Santa a childish note saying I wanted a man for Christmas, and when I woke up the next morning, there he was."

"That doesn't make any sense. Where was he?"

"Asleep under the tree."

She gasped. "Was he naked?"

"Of course he wasn't! Why would you ask that?" I was extremely glad that Ben could only hear my side of the conversation, but judging from his ever widening smile coupled with the heat blazing on my cheeks, I could only assume that he was adept at filling in the blanks.

"I don't know. I must be thinking of Adam and Eve. Maybe Santa didn't have any clothes that fit him. I imagine that everything at the North Pole must be pretty much elf-sized, except for Santa's clothes, and he's probably much too chubby to share . . ."

"Mom, you're rambling!"

"I can't help it. This is just so exciting. My oldest daughter is finally going to get married!"

"Don't you think you're getting a little ahead of your-self?"

"He's a gift, sweetie. It's not like you can just return him. Is he handsome?" she said breathlessly.

"Very."

"I knew it! Is he there now?"

"Yes."

"Put him on! I want to talk to him."

I put my hand over the receiver. "My mother wants to talk to you."

"Sure. Why not?"

"You're about to find out," I said under my breath. "Mom, I'm putting you on speaker."

The line was quiet for a minute before a timid voice said, "Hello?"

"Hello, Mrs. Canfield," Ben boomed. "Merry Christmas."

"Good gracious, it really is a man."

Ben laughed.

"We're so happy to hear your voice, aren't we, Martin?"

I could hear the television in the background, probably football, and my father grunted a non-committal noise that could have been a yes or no.

"Martin!" my mother said shrilly. "This is important. Could you turn that down for a minute?

My dad's voice came over the line next, apologetic. "Merry Christmas, sweetie. Sorry about all the commotion, but the game is on."

"Its okay, Dad; you go watch."

"Not before he talks to . . . I'm terribly sorry, dear, but I didn't catch your name."

"I'm Ben."

"What a nice name—very strong, sturdy. And I can tell from your voice that you're tall. How tall are you, exactly?"

I cut in. "Sorry, Mom. The connection is terrible; I can barely hear you. I'll call you back later."

"It's all right, dear. I'm sure you're anxious to play with your new toy anyway."

"Mom!" I wailed.

"Yes, you heard that, didn't you? I'll let you go. Give me a call when you have a minute."

"Bye, Mom. Bye, Dad."

"Bye, sweetie. And good-bye to you too, Ben, dear. I hope we'll be seeing you very soon."

I hung up my phone, my face burning hot. "I'm sorry you had to hear that. She's usually quite rational, but when she starts to talk about me in a relationship, she suddenly gets this strange, almost manic gleam in her eyes. She's commented on more than one occasion that if I'd just get married, she could die happy."

"Well, she's a parent. What's wrong with that?"

"She's not even sixty yet, and she talks about me fulfilling her dying wish like she might go tomorrow!"

"All parents want to see their children happy."

"What makes you think I'm not happy?"

"Settled, then," he amended.

"I'm about as settled as it gets. I thought talking to them might jog your memory, make you remember something about your own parents."

"Nope—still a complete blank."

"I'm sorry. As crazy as my mother makes me sometimes, I don't know what I would do if she wasn't there." I was silent for a minute, trying to decide how to phrase my next question. "Why do you think no one has come forward to identify you yet?"

"Maybe my family is from farther away than we thought."

"But still, if my husband had just disappeared, I would be frantic. Someone should have noticed that you're gone by now."

"Maybe I'm alone in the world, and you know what that means; no in-laws."

"A strong selling point, indeed, not that you'd have to

sweeten the deal. Any girl would consider herself lucky to be your wife."

"Would you?" he asked, the words hanging in the air between us.

I didn't know what to say. The impetuous haze that had infected my brain earlier had lifted, leaving only the memories of my past failures at love and my strong resolve not to put myself into that position again. Suddenly, it wasn't just a heady game of emotional Scrabble we were engaged in. The words had meanings attached to them that were all too real and much too serious for my liking. I felt threatened, and I retreated.

"You know what? I'm starving. What do you say we close up a little bit early and I'll buy you dinner?"

If Ben was disappointed at my avoidance of his question, he didn't show it. He looked at the clock, raising one eyebrow. "Twenty-five minutes early?"

"What can I say? Tonight I feel like living dangerously."

"I can't let you buy me dinner."

"I think a meal in exchange for a day's work is fair."

He shook his head. "It's too expensive."

I looked down at my clothes which, despite my apron, were covered in flour. "I wasn't exactly talking about fine dining. How about Taco Bell?"

"I suppose that wouldn't be too offensive to my masculine pride."

I pulled the pies out of the oven and left them on the counter to cool. "Let me just grab my coat and we'll go."

"Okay, but I think I should warn you, I can do some serious damage at Taco Bell. After only that sandwich and cookies for lunch, I could probably eat one of everything on the value menu." He held the door for me and I swiveled around on my crutches, giving him a stern look.

"We're not going to start that again, are we?"

Ten

At ten o'clock the next morning, I was still in bed, toasty under my covers. It was Sunday, and I'd been awake for a while, but I hadn't been able to convince myself to venture out yet. My stomach growled, reminding me that it had been a long time since Taco Bell last night.

Over dinner, which included tacos, a burrito, and nachos for Ben and a quesadilla and Diet Pepsi for me, Ben was strangely secretive about his plans for today. I was amused at his sudden tight-lipped stance and a bit intrigued as well.

"I can't tell you," he said.

"C'mon, we've been through a lot together," I pleaded.

"I'm sorry, but it's not up for discussion."

"Have it your way. If you want to have brunch with Veronica What's-her-name, I won't think any less of you. Well, I will, but I wouldn't tell you so."

Ben shook his head good-naturedly. "It's not like that. I just happen to have plans tomorrow, that's all."

"Whatever. I hope the two of you will be very happy together. Just promise you won't tell me about the wedding until it's over, because I'm pretty sure I couldn't stay silent during that part where they ask if anyone has any objections—not with a clear conscience, anyway."

"I'll send you a postcard once we're safely away on our honeymoon."

My growling stomach finally got the best of me, and I rolled out of bed and went into the kitchen to investigate my breakfast options. I decided that there was no harm in putting a roast in the Crock Pot for later, and I told myself that I was cooking a lavish dinner because I deserved it. I really should start taking better care of myself, and what better place to start than with a real Sunday dinner instead of something that required four minutes in the microwave? The other voice in my head said that it was impractical to cook a roast for one person—I'd be eating it for a week if Ben didn't show up, which was really why I was cooking it in the first place. Perhaps if he called or showed up at my door, I could lure him into staying with a home-cooked meal.

After I got the roast started, I toasted myself a bagel, warming my hands over the bright orange heat of the toaster slots. I grabbed the Sunday paper, my buttered bagel, and a mug of cocoa and went back to bed. I had just located the funnies when my phone rang.

"Hello?"

"I'm sorry—did I wake you?" Grace said guiltily.

"No, I'm just in bed, reading the paper."

"Good for you. This is your only day to sleep in, and you should stay in bed all day. I would."

"I couldn't stay in bed indefinitely. This is the only day I have to do normal things. Make breakfast, read the paper . . ."

"—hang out with your new boyfriend?"

"You never give up, do you?"

"If I'm interrupting, I'd be more than happy to call back later."

"I'm just eating my solitary bagel, and Ben isn't here, if that's what you mean."

"Why not?" she demanded.

I choked on a sip of cocoa, spluttering into the phone. "Grace, its ten o'clock on a Sunday morning; why would Ben be here?"

"I don't know. It's not beyond the realm of possibility that you could be having breakfast together before church."

"Somehow, I don't think Ben is really a church kind of guy. But he does like to eat . . ."

"How do you know he's not religious? Come to think of it, how does *he* know?"

"He skipped right over the religion question, and I didn't bring it up again."

"It couldn't hurt to ask him to go to church with you."

"I don't want to make him uncomfortable. Besides, he has plans today. I probably won't even see him." I thought about the roast in the kitchen, simmering away on the counter, a direct contradiction of my supposed nonchalant acceptance.

"What kind of plans could he possibly have?"

"He wouldn't tell me."

"I knew it! He's going out with that tart from the police station."

I laughed. "It's funny, but that's exactly what I accused him of."

"And?"

"He denied it."

"There's nothing funny about it. I don't like this at all. You've got to make more of an effort or someone else is going to snatch him up."

"Grace . . ."

"No, listen. Call Ben and invite him to dinner. I understand that this is the one day of the week that you don't have to cook, so I can see why you would want to stay out of the kitchen. You won't have to do a thing. I'll drop dinner off at your house, and I'll be sneaky. You'll never even know I was there."

"Neither of us needs to go to any trouble. Ben already told me he has plans, and it's not going to hurt for me to go a day without seeing him. It was probably just a polite way of saying that he'd like some time to himself since he's spent every day since Christmas with me."

"What does that tell you? Abbie, he likes you, I know he does. But you have to stop pushing him away."

"I'm not pushing him away, and I'm not going to badger him into coming over when he's already told me he's busy," I said, gritting my teeth before I could add anything else.

"Maybe you could just drop off some dinner at his hotel later . . ."

"Grace . . ." I warned.

"I know, I know, it's none of my business."

"What are you having for dinner?" I asked, trying to steer her onto another topic.

"Roast."

"That sounds nice," I said evenly, trying to keep the smile out of my words.

"You're welcome to come."

"Thanks, but I think I'll just lounge around here, dig something out of the freezer."

"You'd better not slob around in your pajamas all day. Someone might stop by to visit."

"I'm not shy. You've seen me in my pajamas before."

"Ha ha. You know what I meant."

"Honestly, sometimes I swear you sound just like Mom."

I heard Grace gasp on the other end of the line. "YOU TAKE THAT BACK!" she thundered.

I giggled. "I'm sorry, but you had it coming. Remember we always promised to warn each other if we started to exhibit some of Mom's less desirable genes?"

"Yes, but this is different because I'm only trying to be helpful." She still sounded a little miffed, but even through the phone I could tell that she wasn't really angry.

"Give me a break, okay? I'm going to church later, so I'll be fully dressed and presentable. Happy?"

"I suppose. We're having dinner around six, if you change your mind. I'll make plenty, just in case."

"Don't say I didn't warn you when you're eating leftovers all week."

"You know what they say—the way to a man's heart is through his stomach. You should know that better than anyone."

"I love you, but sometimes it's hard to remember why."

"Love you too." She hung up, and I suddenly wanted to call Ben's hotel room, just to see if he would pick up. I wondered if he was still in bed too, or if he was already off on his secret errand. My cocoa was cold now and I pushed it away, forcing myself to concentrate on the paper instead.

✳ ✳ ✳ ✴ ✳ ✳ ✳

The singles ward is an interesting part of the transition to adulthood. I went straight from my home ward to college, and then lived with my parents after I graduated so I could pay off my loans. So I entered the singles ward setting much later her in the game than most of my friends. I always felt like something of a pariah at my singles ward. Well, maybe pariah is the wrong word. I'm not exactly an outcast, but I don't really fit in with the other girls either, probably because I'm at least five years older than most of them. I guess I'm more of a den mother. My house is really close to the family ward I grew up in, and the first week I attended my new singles ward, I made a disturbing discovery. There were three or four girls that I recognized from Young Women, only instead of being their classmate, I used to be their teacher. How was it possible that they were old enough to be attending a singles ward? Surely it was only yesterday that I was reprimanding them as chatty little thirteen-year-old Beehives for talking in my class. Their faces were bright with youth and hope, and although I'm not aged enough to fit into the old crone category yet, they had a vitality and zest that I could only look back on fondly. They had not yet seen enough of the world to be jaded, and I envied them their innocence.

This was to say nothing of the male population of the

ward, which consisted mainly of boys on the brink of leaving on missions, looking for someone to write to them like love-sick puppies, and the ones who'd just returned—they were the chief focus of my little flock of former Young Women. The girls sat in clusters, whispering furiously and giggling while the guys sat in ones, twos, and threes, trying to look cool and disinterested, all the while knowing that they were being blatantly sized up. The fact that everyone knew they were there to meet their companion for not only this life but the rest of eternity was the proverbial elephant in the room so huge that it was impossible to avoid talking about.

When I first started going there, I was nervous most of the time. It seemed that we all came every week to play a game, one that I suspected everyone else had been given the rules to before I arrived; everyone knew the secret handshake but me. But once I decided to stop looking for my soul mate, I was able to concentrate on other things. I could listen to a speaker and actually get something out of his talk, instead of wondering if he was looking at me or the girl one row back. It might sound unreasonable, but take the whole romance thing out of the equation, and your average singles ward is an entirely different experience. I made a few friends in the ward, girls and boys, but they all seemed to look at me as some sort of wise, older sister. Secretly I was relieved when I turned thirty and moved into the more mature singles ward, for the "seasoned" members. At least I didn't feel like such an old lady anymore.

No more did I flounder and perspire, hoping desperately that this would be the week that someone new would show up. I used to have it all planned out in my mind. He would be tall, well-dressed, and mysterious, maybe even with some kind of accent. And he'd be my age, of course, and he would sit on the back row by himself because he didn't know anyone. Everyone else would be intimidated by him because of his brooding good looks—everyone but me. I would walk back and sit next to him and introduce myself, (because in this particular fantasy I am incredibly confident and self-assured), and he would smile. He would tell me his name, his cool accent (maybe English . . . or Scottish) rolling off his tongue with an impish charm. We would shake hands warmly, and something would jolt through both of us. There would be honest-to-goodness sparks, and every girl in the room would wish, just for a minute, that she was me.

That was in the past. I had put all those foolish notions of impossibly romantic scenarios behind me now. There would be no mystery man appearing out of nowhere and sweeping me off my feet because I was in complete control of my destiny.

Until today.

I sat on the back row, listening to the prelude music and waiting for sacrament meeting to start, wearing an outfit I still wasn't quite sure about. Mostly I wear dark, sensible colors; blacks, browns, and grays. On a whim, I bought this filmy lavender skirt on clearance last summer. It really wasn't me, but I loved the color. It reminded me of a lilac bush my grandmother used to have. It was one of those impulse buys that end up at the back of your closet, never again to see the light of day, and I wouldn't have been wearing it now if I hadn't forgotten to pick up my three best skirts from the dry cleaners yesterday.

For one thing, it was out of season. The flimsy layers were obviously made for the hottest days of summer, thus dooming me to spend three hours in the drafty church in December, freezing to death. Add to that my improbable shoe selection-the only thing I could find that went with the skirt was a pair of white, strappy sandals. Well, one strappy sandal; the injured foot could only watch jealously, still stuck in its protective boot. I had to tiptoe through the obstacle course of snow drifts and black ice in the parking lot, and I almost didn't make it up the stairs with my crutches. I don't know what I was thinking. I looked like someone who goes on a tropical vacation expecting sun and sand, only to discover that the island had suffered a freak snowstorm.

As I was contemplating going home to change, I noticed a commotion in the group of girls directly in front of me. They were staring, not very discreetly, at someone who had just come through the lobby doors. From where I was sitting, I could not yet see whoever it was, but judging from the attention the person was eliciting, he or she must have been quite a spectacle. I could only guess from past experience that either some poor girl had made an unfortunate choice regarding a very short skirt and thigh-high boots or there was a hot new guy in our midst.

It didn't take me long to figure out it was the latter scenario that had captured everyone's interest. Looking at it from my detached perspective, it all seemed like such an elaborate hoax. I watched with a note of amusement, wondering why I had ever subjected myself to the whole charade in the first place. To be honest, I felt above it all now. I don't care if it sounds smug—I watched those eager girls with a feeling of what can only be described as superiority, for I had transcended the need for a man's approval. I told myself how much better it was now, to be a spectator instead of a participant. I wouldn't trade places with one of those swooning girls for all the tea in China. I sat back and folded my arms across my chest, ready to watch the carnage unfold, firm in the knowledge of my neutrality. I was Switzerland.

Until I saw his face.

Watching him in profile, searching the pews, my heart thumped almost painfully when I realized that it was Ben. It was Ben, and he was looking for me. This new discovery caused my heart to stumble again, tripping over itself like someone who is relearning the skill of walking. I realized that I was gripping the arm of the bench fiercely, my knuckles white with the strain, and I forced myself to fold my hands in my lap, desperate to retain at least the appearance of calm.

Ben finally spotted me and our eyes locked, but only for a second. He lowered his gaze almost shyly and made his way across the chapel to me. All the while, my heart was continuing to surprise me with its new routine of skips and jumps. It seemed that it had remembered how it was supposed to behave and was currently bouncing along at double the previous rate, trying to make up for lost time.

When he finally reached me, he smiled and said simply, "Is this seat taken?"

I mimicked his smile graciously, gesturing with an open hand. "Go ahead. I'm not expecting anyone."

Ben settled in a respectable distance away from me, putting out his hand for me to shake. "I'm Ben," he said, gripping my hand firmly.

"Abbie," I said in return, feeling the temperature in the room climb ten degrees.

"It's nice to meet you, Abbie," he said, his grin wider now, as if he hadn't enjoyed himself this much in quite some time. I, on the other hand, was starting to sweat in a very un-neutral-like manner.

Switzerland, indeed.

✳ ✳ ✳ ✵ ✳ ✳ ✳

"You look like a flower," Ben whispered as the prelude music abruptly stopped.

A laugh exploded before I could stop it, and I clapped a hand across my mouth before any more of it could escape. Ben coughed, his face beet red.

"Is that your best pick-up line? I never knew you were such a smooth talker," I said quietly, trying to prevent another outburst of laughter.

"That's not what I meant," he said, clearly frustrated. He focused those chocolate brown eyes on me intently. "Everyone in this room is the same—drab, like winter. But you stand out. You look like spring."

My mouth was half open, but my next words died on my lips, which was just as well since the bishop was starting to speak anyway. How did Ben always know the thing to say that would rattle me the most?

"What are you doing here?" I said in a low voice during the announcements, hoping that I sounded nonchalant.

"You know, it seems like every time we meet, you ask me the same question. A less determined man might have taken offense and given up by now."

"I meant, how did you know I would be here?"

"Well, a little bird told me where your ward was and what time to be here."

"That little bird wouldn't happen to answer to the name Grace, would it?"

"The little bird in question wished to remain anonymous, and I have a responsibility to protect my sources."

I surveyed him, giving him my most dangerous look. "We can do this the easy way or the hard way; it's completely up to you."

"It was Grace," he said quickly. "I warned her that I'd never be able to hold up under interrogation."

"Remind me not to tell you any of my earth-shattering secrets. You folded like a little girl."

"I couldn't help it. I was afraid you might force feed me that chocolate mousse cake until I talked."

We sat next to each other in relative silence, but I was not oblivious to the buzzing of everyone around us, and it appeared that Ben had caught the furtive glances and sly whispering as well.

"Is something special happening today?" he hissed into my ear.

"How very perceptive of you to notice."

"Well? Are you going to let me in on the secret?"

"The special thing happening today is you."

"What?"

"You are what everyone is talking about."

"But they don't even know me."

"That makes you even more appealing."

"I don't understand."

I sighed. "Obviously, you're new to the world of singles wards, so I'll have to spell it out for you. You are a handsome, new (and therefore exciting), well-dressed stranger with no apparent attachments who has wandered into an unsuspecting flock of hungry predators. To them, you are the equivalent of fresh meat."

"I guess it's lucky I have you here to make sure no one takes advantage of the situation."

"You have no idea." I started to relax a little bit, leaning back against the bench. I was feeling slightly guilty; obviously Ben was here because Grace had pressured him into coming. The sacrament hymn was starting, and I leaned over to Ben, whispering in his ear. "You know, it's very sweet of you to come, but you really don't have to stay. I know you had plans today."

Ben took my hand, and an audible collective gasp rose from the girls sitting in the row across from us. "Abbie, these *were* my plans for today," he said, squeezing my hand momentarily before releasing it. "No need to give the gossip mongers any more ammunition than is absolutely necessary," he added.

Ben seemed very well versed in the LDS Church meeting scenario. Other than not taking the sacrament, he did every-thing else like a pro. In fact, I came to the conclusion that either he could adapt incredibly well to new environments, or he must be a member. When the closing prayer was over, I turned to him. I felt a little self-conscious, as if we really had met for the first time only an hour ago. It was like I was seeing a completely different side of him, and despite Grace's powers of persuasion, I wondered if his coming to church was strictly for my benefit. Ben stood expectantly, and I joined him. I didn't know quite where to go from there. Suddenly, we were back on the steps of the police station on Christmas Day, with Ben waiting patiently for me to lead the way.

"I'm really glad you came," I said finally, my eyes never quite reaching his, instead lingering at his ocean blue tie. "It

gets lonely sitting on the back row by myself." I felt completely out of my comfort zone, and I suddenly panicked at the
thought of having to make conversation if I asked him back to
my house for dinner. I needed some time to think about recent
developments, so I took the coward's way out. "Can I drop
you off at your hotel?"

"If I'm not mistaken, you have two meetings left. You
weren't thinking of sneaking out early, were you?" he said,
like he was a stern parent confronting a child whose arm was
buried to the elbow in the cookie jar.

I stared at him in amazement. "Did Grace give you a crash
course in the Mormon faith?"

The bishop suddenly appeared at my side. "Abbie, it's good
to see you today. Would you like to introduce me to your
friend?"

"This is Ben," I said.

"It's great to meet you, Ben. Are you new in town?" the
bishop said as they shook hands.

"Very new; in fact, I just arrived on Christmas Eve."

"Really? And what brings you to our area?"

"I was helping Santa with a special project," he said, beam-
ing at me.

I rolled my eyes.

"Well, Abbie, this all sounds very mysterious. How did
you and Ben meet?"

"I was . . . involved with the project as well."

"I think that's great. Nothing will get you in the Christmas
spirit like service to others. So, how long are you going to be
with us, Brother . . . ?"

"It's just Ben," I said quickly.

"Brother . . . Ben . . ." the bishop trailed off.

"I'm not really sure. There are still some loose ends I need
to tie up."

"Excellent. Well, we hope to see much more of you,
Brother Ben. I'd be happy to walk you to the next meeting, if
you'd like. I know it's a bit unusual, but we have Priesthood

before Sunday School. It seems to be the only way to keep everyone from sneaking out early," he said, winking.

Ben nodded. "Abbie, I'll see you in a while, okay?"

I stepped closer, keeping my voice quiet as the bishop waited. "I don't want you to feel like you have to go."

"Well, I can hardly go with you to the girl meeting."

"You know that's not what I meant. We can leave, if you want."

He looked into my face, and although his lips were smiling, his eyes were serious. "Don't worry, Abbie. I know what I'm doing."

At least one of us did.

Ben and I had definitely had our moments, times when I thought for sure that he was one of the good ones. But watching him amble off to Priesthood meeting, I knew for the first time that I was in real trouble.

✳ ✳ ✳ ✳ ✳ ✳ ✳

By the time I'd rejoined Ben for Sunday School, I was feeling a little more in control. I'm ashamed to say that I couldn't tell you anything about the lesson from Relief Society. I had spent the entire time giving myself a mental pep talk. I reasoned that since Ben had gone to all the trouble of tracking me down and going to church with me, the least I could do was feed him.

After the meeting, we walked to the glass doors in the foyer, watching as the sky disappeared in a dismal mass of puffy gray clouds that seemed to be gathering as we stood there.

"I'll take you up on that offer for the ride now, if you're still willing," Ben said. "It's starting to look pretty hostile out there."

"What if I said we had to take a little detour first?"

"What did you have in mind?"

"I thought you might like to have a nice, home-cooked

Sunday dinner with me before I drop you off."

"That's my favorite kind of detour. Would it be rude of me to ask what we're having?"

"Would it make a difference?"

"Heck, no. You're looking at a guy who was planning on dinner from the vending machine outside the hotel."

"What would that have been, I wonder?"

"Probably a couple of those little packages with a stick of meat and a stick of cheese, and some chips, and a Sprite, and maybe a Snickers or a fruit pie for dessert."

"You said that almost like you've been looking forward to it."

"Well, that depends. Why don't you tell me what you're serving and I'll weigh my options."

"Whatever. That sad collection of items you just mentioned does not qualify as a meal. In fact, I think in several countries it would constitute cruel and unusual punishment."

"Now you're just exaggerating. You've got your meat and dairy group, and the potato chips count as a vegetable. Sprite has lemon *and* lime, and the fruit pie adds another fruit serving. It's very nutritionally sound."

"Just because they call it a fruit pie doesn't mean there is any actual fruit in it. It's just . . . fruit flavored sugary goop," I argued, pulling into my driveway. "Why didn't you tell me you were running out of money? I could buy you some groceries, you know. No one should have to live off vending machine fare."

"I have plenty of money left, but thank you for the offer," he said, holding the door to my house open for me.

The savory smell of roast beef wafted up to meet us, and Ben inhaled appreciatively. I stopped, turning to face him. "I don't get it. If you have money, why were you going to eat junk for dinner?"

He shrugged. "It was convenient."

I pushed him toward the kitchen. "Obviously you've forgotten what real food is like, and trust me when I say that it's worth the effort." I switched off the roast and poured the remaining juices into a pan for gravy.

"What can I do?" Ben asked.

"You don't have to do anything."

"I'm not actually being gallant. I'm starving and I'll do whatever I can to help get the food ready faster."

"My hero. Well, you can peel potatoes."

Ben unbuttoned his cuffs and rolled up his sleeves. He picked up a potato and began expertly removing the skin with a paring knife. "I'm a really speedy potato peeler. In fact, I was voted most likely to peel potatoes in high school."

I snorted. "You were not."

"I can't really remember. It sounded good, though."

"I bet you were one of those popular football jocks in high school."

"Is that a good thing or a bad thing?"

"That depends. Did you use your powers for good or evil?"

"Actually, I didn't go to high school."

I wiped my hands on a dishtowel, surveying him skeptically. "Oh, really?"

"Yup, my parents were circus performers. We traveled all over the country with the circus. We were never in the same place for more than a week, so I didn't go to school."

"What did your parents do in the circus, exactly?" I said, deciding to play along.

"They were the trapeze act. It was really dangerous, and the crowd loved it because they refused to use a net. I can remember several occasions where I was nearly orphaned."

"What was your skill?"

"Well, for a while, I showed incredible promise as a lion tamer. The trick is to never show fear. As long as the lions are convinced that you believe you're in charge, they roll over and purr just like kittens."

"So, what happened?" Despite the fact that I knew that Ben was making it up as he went along, I was genuinely curious.

"As it turns out, I was allergic."

"Come on."

"Yeah, you know—cats and lions are from the same family; same genes."

"Same fur," I added.

"Exactly."

"Then what was your talent? Fire eating? Juggling?"

"Allergic to those too, I'm afraid. No, I was the bearded man."

I laughed out loud. "I thought most circuses had a bearded lady."

He shook his head. "Ours got a better offer from a rival circus and she left. They had a really hard time trying to replace her; apparently, bearded ladies are fairly difficult to come by. Meanwhile, my parents were getting a little embarrassed, since everything circus-related that I'd tried so far gave me watery eyes and sneezing fits. So when I hit puberty and my beard grew in, they talked the manager into letting me go onstage as the bearded man. For some reason, no one applauded."

"That is a very sad story."

"What can I say? I have no marketable qualities."

"I very much doubt that. You're an excellent potato peeler, at any rate," I said, unable to conceal the amusement that had crept into my tone. "You peeled the entire bag. How many people did you think were going to be joining us?"

"I'm sorry. I got so involved with my circus story that I just kept going. You should have told me to stop. How was I supposed to know how many potatoes you needed?"

"I figured it was common sense. Never mind, we'll just have leftovers."

"I doubt it. I love mashed potatoes, and I'm really, really hungry."

"Even you can't eat an entire bag's worth of mashed potatoes."

"Want to bet?"

✳ ✳✳ ✴ ✳ ✳

An hour and four heaping mounds of mashed potatoes later, Ben leaned back in his chair, patting his stomach contentedly. "I must say, that was a delicious dinner. It made my vending machine plans look very pathetic. I don't know what I would have done if Santa had dropped me down someone else's chimney. You've taken such good care of me."

I blushed a little. "I didn't do much. Any single girl with eyes would have done the same."

"No, I don't think so," he said, his voice suddenly quiet and serious. "I've never met anyone quite like you, Abbie."

"You have amnesia. For all you know, you've met any number of girls like me."

"No, I know."

"How do you know?"

"I just do," he said simply.

"I have to ask—what did you mean at church when you said you knew what you were doing?"

He paused, considering his words carefully. "When we were sitting in that meeting, I felt something. I had the distinct impression that I'd been there before."

"I'm pretty sure I would remember if you'd been there before."

"I didn't mean literally. There was just something so . . . familiar about it. It was almost like going home. I don't know— maybe I just felt that way because you were there." He grinned lopsidedly as if he was a shy child, freely giving a gift while at the same time not knowing if it would be rejected.

I felt a lump appear in my throat suddenly, and I found myself thinking, why not? Why not just give in and accept what is being offered? What could it hurt to just relax my guard, just this once? Competing with that voice was one that was equally persuasive, if not more so. It warned me that no one was that caring; no one available, at least. There was nothing to gain and potentially everything to lose if I let myself feel something for Ben.

He was looking across the table at me earnestly as his hand drifted slowly to mine, tentatively covering it with his. But it was too much. My senses were on emotional overload, and his gesture overwhelmed me. I pulled my hand away awkwardly.

"I'm sorry," he said, his voice laced with regret.

"Don't be. You have nothing to be sorry for."

"What is it?" he asked.

"It just isn't right."

"What isn't right?"

"This. Us," I said in frustration, trying to find the right words. "All we can be is friends because you already belong to someone else."

"You don't know that."

"But it's very possible. And until you remember who you are and where you belong, that's how it has to stay."

Ben hesitated. He took a deep breath. "Abbie," he started.

My phone rang. I took a quick peek at the caller ID. "It's Grace. She's probably wondering why I never showed up for dinner."

"Aren't you going to get it?"

"It's okay. I'll let the voicemail get it. I can call her back later. What were you going to say?"

Before he could say anything, the phone began to ring again. I frowned. "It's Grace again."

"You'd better see what she wants."

I gave Ben an apologetic look. "Hello?"

"Hey, are you busy?" Grace asked, in a rush.

"Why, is something wrong?"

"Sort of. Hannah has a high fever, and I'm worried. Would you mind coming over and keeping an eye on the other kids while Jack and I take her to the ER?

"Of course, it's no trouble. I'll be right there."

"Is everything okay?" Ben asked.

"Hannah has a fever. Grace wants me to come over and

stay with Morgan and Jake while she and Jack take Hannah to the hospital."

"I'll go with you," he offered.

"You don't have to. I don't know how late I'll be there."

"It's not like I've got anyplace to be."

I shrugged. "If you really want to . . ."

"Let's go."

I grabbed my coat and crutches, locking the door behind us. "I'm sorry, you wanted to say something, but we got interrupted."

"Don't worry about it; it wasn't important."

I was concerned about Hannah, and I didn't bother arguing with him.

✴ ✴ ✴ ✴ ✴ ✴ ✴

Although Grace looked tired and worried, she perked up a little when she saw Ben with me. "This is so nice of you guys. I'm sorry I interrupted your evening. There are leftovers from dinner in the fridge, if you're interested."

"Normally, I never turn down food, but your sister wouldn't let me leave the table until I finished off the roast and mashed potatoes."

"Really?" Grace said. "I thought you were just going to rummage in the freezer for something quick and easy?"

"I did. The roast came from the freezer, and everyone knows there's nothing easier than the Crock Pot."

"Did you find the mashed potatoes in the freezer too?"

Jack came down the stairs with a pink-cheeked, wobbly Hannah, saving me from any further inquiries. "Hey, look at you; wearing clothes," Jack said, greeting Ben. Ben only grinned.

"Hi, Aunt Abbie," Hannah said, her voice small and scratchy.

I kissed her warm forehead. "Hello, Hannah Banana."

"We'll be back as soon as we can," Grace said.

"No rush, we'll be fine," Ben assured her.

On the way out the door, Hannah called out, "No fair. You guys are going to have fun without me."

"I promise we won't have any fun until you get back," I said.

We popped popcorn and watched *Finding Nemo* with Morgan and Jake. I threatened to cut off their Slurpee supply if they ever told Hannah we had fun. Grace and Jack came home late. Hannah was asleep in Jack's arms, and he carried her up and tucked her in. I told Grace that I would try to come by tomorrow night with some strawberry ice cream for Hannah, whose rapid strep test came back positive.

I dropped Ben off at his hotel, thanking him for being such a good sport. As I drove home, I wondered idly how the night might have been different, had we continued our conversation uninterrupted. I got into bed quickly, wanting to get a few hours sleep before I had to open the bakery in the morning. I was still thinking about what Ben might have said next when I drifted off to sleep.

Eleven

I glanced at the clock for what had to be the twentieth time, and that was just in the last hour.

11:25 AM.

I sighed. It had been a long day already. The minute I got to the bakery, I had launched into a series of time-consuming recipes. I had the toffee chocolate chip cookie recipe in my hand before I even took my coat off. I hardly ever make them anymore because I like them too much. In fact, I noticed I was steering people toward buying other things, just so I could be assured of the leftovers. It was probably a mistake to make them today, but I was beyond caring. I needed comfort food.

I couldn't help thinking about my conversation with Ben after dinner, wondering what it was he didn't say. If only my phone had rung three minutes later. I kept rewinding it in my head; my breath catching as I remembered the earnest look on his face when he said he'd never met anyone like me.

There was something wrong with me today. My stomach was churning, and my face was flushed. There were two possibilities; I was coming down with the flu, or I was in love. I guess it could also have something to do with the four cookies I'd eaten already this morning.

It must be the flu. I couldn't be in love. I didn't do love anymore. And as much as Ben might think he was interested

now, surely it was only a matter of time before a flash of rec-
ognition would send him running in the direction of his other
life.

What I needed more than anything else was to keep busy.
No good could come of letting my mind dwell on fruitless
possibilities. After the cookies, I made cranberry orange scones
and sugar doughnuts before moving on to a rather ambitious
Black Forest cake, which was in the oven now. The delicious
aroma of browned chocolate wafted from the oven. I kept
myself busy whipping the cream by hand with a whisk. No
use wasting all this pent-up energy when I could be undoing
some of the caloric damage from the cookies.

All morning, I found my heart in my throat every time the
bell on the door rang. I would take a deep breath before putting on a smile that I hoped could overcome the nervousness,
squaring my shoulders, and walking out to face Ben as bravely
as if I were going into battle.

But it was never him. Over the course of the morning,
my emotions had run the gamut from panic and anxiety to
impatience before settling on despair. I knew I had dropped
him off kind of late, but I really thought he'd be here by now.
For days now, I hadn't been able to shake him, and suddenly,
he'd inexplicably disappeared. Despite all efforts to the con-
trary, I was starting to become dependent on him. The lonely,
pathetic part of me whimpered, wondering why Ben was staying away. The independent part of me confidently assured the
lonely, pathetic part that we were fine without Ben. And the
neurotic, worrywart part of me questioned whether he might
have been hit by a bus. In short, I was a wreck.

To top it all off, the weather was not cooperating. The sky
began as an innocuous gray but was quickly morphing into a
full-blown, blustery nightmare. It was making me even more
nervous, if that was possible. I've never been much of a snow
person. While I admit that the white stuff is a necessary part of
catching the Christmas spirit, my feelings wouldn't be hurt if
spring began on December 26. It's nice to watch when you're

next to a cozy fire, but I hate driving in it, and shoveling it is an exercise in futility, as far as I'm concerned. Not only is it chilly and wet, but the minute you got the driveway cleared, another batch flies in to replace it and you have to start all over again.

The bell clanged on the door, and I glanced around the corner in time to see Iris, doing a little cold dance as the door shut behind her. I groaned audibly.

"Hey, Abbie. I'm happy to see you too," she said, unwinding her scarf.

"It's not that. I've been waiting for someone all day."

She gave me a curious look. "Who are you waiting for?"

I flushed. I hadn't really intended to give out that much information. "The mailman. I'm waiting for a . . . package to be delivered," I finished lamely.

"Oh. I thought you might be waiting for the gorgeous guy that was hanging on your every word the other day."

"I don't know what you're talking about." I had a bowl of brownie batter in my arms, and I stirred it furiously.

"Come on, you don't need to be coy with me. I'm totally happy for you."

"I'm not being coy. Ben and I are just friends."

"Right."

"We are," I said defensively. "And when his wife comes looking for him, I will have nothing to feel guilty about, and no broken heart."

"Abbie, there is no wife—there can't be. The two of you belong together!"

"But if he's already married, it doesn't matter." I realized that the muscles in my arm were starting to ache from the punishment I was inflicting on the batter. I set it down on the counter and blew out a frustrated breath.

Iris surveyed the bowl. "Are those brownies?"

"They will be when they grow up."

She frowned. "You stirred them so long you'll probably be able to use them to re-shingle your roof."

I glared at her. "Who's the chef here—you or me?"

She merely smiled serenely.

"It's your fault anyway for steering me onto such a maddening topic."

"Ooh," she said, hovering over the glass case. "Sugar doughnuts! These are my favorite and you never make them. What's the occasion?"

"My keen psychic abilities told me that you might be stopping by this morning."

"Are you sure it isn't because Ben likes sugar doughnuts?"

"I have no idea what Ben's feelings are on doughnuts, sugar or otherwise," I huffed.

"Just checking. I'll take two. I like the way the sugar sticks to my lips."

The comment was so unexpected that I couldn't help chuckling. "Me too." I put two doughnuts in a white paper sack for her.

Iris scanned the case. "*And* you made scones. It's like you're expecting the queen to drop by or perhaps just . . . Prince Charming?"

"Cut it out. I was just feeling ambitious today, that's all. I'm halfway through a Black Forest cake, if you want to hang around."

Her eyes got big. "You are the diet devil. The weather's getting icky, and since there's no one here to ogle, I think I'll go while I still have a waistline left to salvage."

By noon, the snow was starting to coat the ground. By one, it was actually blowing sideways. The customers were nonexistent, and I knew that soon I would have to start thinking about shoveling. And still there was no sign of Ben. What if he'd remembered who he was and, in his excitement to get home, hadn't even stopped to say good-bye?

I decided to put off the unpleasant task of shoveling a little longer. The layers were cool now, so I busied myself assembling the Black Forest cake. I draped it with clouds of fluffy whipped cream and dotted it with cherries. I also grated milk chocolate for the top instead of my usual dark, telling myself it had nothing to do with hoping a certain someone might want to eat it. As I was sprinkling the chocolate shavings, I glanced out the window. I was alarmed to see that the snow was sticking much faster than I thought. There had to be at least five inches.

I looked down at my injured, open-toed, boot-covered foot. This was going to be more difficult than I expected. I covered my leg to the knee with a garbage bag and abandoned my crutches, layering on the extra clothes I came in before hobbling out to face the weather. After standing in the heated kitchen all morning, the sudden chill hit me like a wall of ice, and I nearly went back inside, resigned to stay put and survive on cookies until it melted.

My foot appeared to be staying fairly dry, and it only throbbed a little. I could put my weight on it pretty well, and after a while it got so cold that I really couldn't feel it anymore. I wasn't sure if that was a good thing or a bad thing. I dug the shovel into a snowdrift, dismayed to discover that the snow was very wet and heavier than it looked. I made my way slowly down the sidewalk, pausing occasionally to rest my foot and survey my progress. My little parking lot had never seemed so massive. I wanted to cry, seeing how much there was left, but I pressed forward, shoveling for what seemed like hours. The fluffy flakes rested on my arms, adding to the bulk of my layers. I imagined I must look quite amusing; a snowman shoveling snow. I could almost see the funny side of the situation, and it was then that I made the mistake of looking behind me.

The sidewalk that I had so meticulously unearthed was covered again.

It was difficult to tell what time it was or how long I'd been outside, as the sky had been the same threatening shade for hours. I hadn't seen a soul since Iris left. I briefly entertained the thought that I might be the last person on the planet, concluding that if I had just spent my last remaining hours on earth shoveling snow instead of having a free-for-all with the desserts, I was going to be even crankier. How long could it possibly keep up like this? The weatherman had forecasted a few flakes, but this was getting ridiculous. It was very easy to feel sorry for myself at that moment. I seemed to be the only girl in the neighborhood who had neither a husband nor a snow blower. And it was at that precise moment that Ben came strolling across the street.

Well, not exactly strolling. The snow was too deep for strolling; it was more like trudging. "Abbie? Is that you?" he called out.

All my warm, fuzzy feelings about him earlier vanished, quickly replaced by anger and recrimination. The weather had drained all my patience. Even though I knew it was none of my business, I wondered what he'd been doing all day. "Of course it's me. Who else would it be?"

"Well, it's hard to tell under all that snow. And how many outfits are you wearing exactly?"

I was in no mood for light banter. "The buses can't be running in this. How did you get here?"

"I walked."

I blanched. "It's way too far. You shouldn't be out in this weather."

"I was about to tell you the same thing. I'd be willing to bet that foot isn't ready to be walked on yet."

"I didn't really have much of a choice."

"Well, you do now. Here, let me do that," he said, reaching for my shovel.

"It's okay, I only have one shovel."

"I only need one shovel."

"I'm just fine, thanks," I said stubbornly.

"Look, I'll shovel, and you can go inside and bake a cake or something."

"I already baked a cake. I baked lots of things today." The end of the sentence came out as rather irrational and unnecessary, but I could feel the fury building and I had never been accused of being the Queen of the Rational Argument once my temper took over.

"Why won't you let me do this for you?" Ben persisted.

"Because it's not your responsibility."

"No one said anything about responsibility. I was just trying to be nice."

"And the court recognizes your niceness as Exhibit A."

He paused. "Are you sure you're Abbie under there?"

"Last time I checked."

"I'm really confused. Maybe you can help me out here. Did I do something wrong?"

I stopped and leaned on my shovel, exasperated. "Why?"

Ben's eyes actually registered hurt. "Because you're acting like you can barely tolerate me."

I wanted to kick myself for being so mean and I probably would have, if I hadn't been too tired to raise my leg. I tried to swallow my bad mood and be pleasant. "It's not that. It was really sweet of you to come by and offer to help, but I'd rather just do it by myself."

"Don't be silly," he said, making a grab at my shovel. In a move of dexterity that surprised me more than Ben, I tossed the shovel into my other hand, holding it where he couldn't reach. "Why are you being like this?" he asked.

"You won't always be here," I said finally.

"What?"

I couldn't bear to look into his sad eyes any longer, so I began throwing shovelfuls of snow as fast as I could while I ranted. "I can't let myself get used to you being nice to me because when you leave, it will be too hard. I'm okay now doing things for myself because I don't know any other way. But if I let you help me, it will be much worse when you go away because I'll know what I'm missing. I'd rather just leave things the way they are." I could barely catch my breath now, huffing and puffing from the shoveling and the tirade.

Ben looked perplexed, as if he were still trying to follow my convoluted logic. He put his hand on my arm, forcing me to pause in my crazed shoveling. "Abbie, I was just offering to shovel snow. You're over thinking this."

I felt sudden tears burning the corners of my eyes, but I pushed them away. I refused to use up my last shred of cred-ibility by crying, since Ben probably thought I was psychotic already. Every muscle in my body was stiff and sore, and all I wanted was to crawl into bed and come out when the sun was back. Ben gave me an encouraging look as he reached for the shovel, but I shook my head.

"I can't do this. Before you came, I was alone, but it was okay. I'd forgotten there could be any other way. Now I'm just confused."

"There is room in your life for someone else, isn't there?"

"I don't know anymore."

"We don't have to decide that now. This is just about you letting someone else do something for you." He gently took the shovel from my hand, and I let him. "Now, I suggest that you go inside and get some work done."

I hesitated for a moment. "I don't need to bake anyway. It will just get wasted. No one is going to come out in this weather."

"Then why were you worried about shoveling?"

I shrugged. "I have to do it sometime. I can't exactly count on the sun coming out to melt it all for me. I can't count on anything or anyone but me."

"That's an awfully lonely way to look at life."

"Maybe, but if I'm the only one I rely on, I'll never be disappointed."

The atmosphere had gotten too serious. "Well, go on, slacker," Ben joked, his eyes warm against the cold sky. "Unless you want to watch."

I couldn't help returning his smile. I began hobbling toward the bakery. Now that I had stopped working, my foot was starting to hurt again. I gasped as it suddenly twisted underneath me. I nearly dropped straight to the ground, but suddenly there were strong arms holding me up. I turned my head sideways, finding my eyes level with Ben's. They were filled with concern and something else I hesitated to define.

"Careful," he said softly, as my frozen breath collided with his. He held me longer than he needed to, finally placing me back on my feet. I managed to make it inside without any further incident and fell into the nearest chair. I felt wobbly, and I wondered how much of that was really from the exertion of my chore. I guessed that Ben's sudden proximity probably had more to do with my spaghetti legs than shoveling ever could. I wasn't mad at him anymore. I wasn't even sure I had ever been angry with him in the first place. I think I was more upset with myself for pining over him all morning. I was beginning to think of him as a permanent fixture in my life, and the sooner I changed that mindset, the better things would be . . . for both of us.

But what if he does stay? a small voice in my head asked.

I was startled by how much I wanted to believe that was a possibility.

When I was feeling sturdy enough to stand, I went into the kitchen and dished up a big piece of the Black Forest cake. I sat in a chair facing the window, watching Ben throw endless piles of snow as if they weighed nothing more than air. I hoped that the cake would convey to him the feelings I couldn't seem to put into words.

Twelve

I was sitting at the bakery counter pouring confetti into little bags when the phone rang.

"You didn't call me once yesterday." Grace's voice was pouty. "Don't you love me anymore?"

"I'm sorry, I was really busy." I cradled the phone between my ear and my neck, trying to tie a bow on one of the bags.

"Oh? Well, if you were occupied with Ben, I suppose I can forgive you."

"I was busy baking and shoveling snow, actually."

"Yeah, what with your foot and all, I almost came by myself to help, but I figured someone else might have taken care of that for you."

"Yes, well, he did shovel snow when he got here, but only because I couldn't talk him out of it."

"Why were you trying to talk him out of it?"

"Because I can take care of myself."

"You know, sometimes you can be insanely frustrating."

"Mmm," I said, noncommittally.

"What are you doing now?"

"I'm getting ready for the party tomorrow." I always had a big party at the bakery on New Year's Eve, as sort of a thank you to my customers. People really seemed to enjoy it, but it was a lot of work. Everyone was invited, all the food was free, and I closed right after midnight. Usually I started getting ready a lot earlier, but this year, I'd been spending so much time with Ben that I'd almost forgotten about it. It was going to be a stretch to get everything ready in time.

"And where is Ben?"

"He's out picking up some last minute things I needed."

"So, he's running your errands now? That's very nice of him."

"Yes, it is. Plus, I needed to get him out of here for a while. He's starting to make me nervous."

"Why?" she said, her voice brightening.

"Never mind. What are you doing today?"

"I was actually calling to see if I could come by for lunch."

I glanced at my wristwatch. 1:16. Where had the morning gone? "I really wish I could, but I have so much to get finished."

"I made chicken salad."

My stomach growled in approval. Grace made the world's best chicken salad. "You win."

✳ ✳✳✴✳✳ ✳

"I promise we'll eat quick and then I'll help you until Ben gets back." Grace patted the paper lunch sack she was carrying.

"You're too good to me. I'm starving," I said as she unwrapped a sandwich and passed it to me. She took a sandwich also, but the bag still looked suspiciously full. "Grace, I know I said I was hungry, but exactly how many sandwiches did you bring?"

"The rest are for Ben."

I shook my head slowly. "You are shameless."

"I hope that we'll be able to come tomorrow night, but it kind of depends on Hannah. Even though she's starting to feel better, I don't want to keep her out too late."

"I understand. If you can't, there's always next year."

"Yeah, but I know what a big deal it is for you." She paused. "Is Ben coming?"

"He said he might stop by."

"I bet he's here at midnight, just in time to see the ball drop. In fact, if I'm not mistaken, I think you might start the New Year with a kiss."

"It's not like that," I stammered, my face turning thirty shades of red. "He wouldn't dare."

"Which is exactly why you should make the first move. I've seen the way he looks at you, but he can't be expected to read your mind . . ."

"Can we please change the subject?"

"Fair enough, I guess." She took a bite of her sandwich, chewing thoughtfully. "So, why is Ben starting to make you nervous?"

"What?" I said, pretending I didn't know what she was referring to.

"Come on, did you really think I was going to just let that slide?"

I hurriedly took a bite of the sandwich so that my mouth could be busy with something other than talking. "This is really good," I mumbled. "And your hair looks so pretty, Gracie. Did you just get it cut?"

"Nice try. Now, answer the question."

I set the sandwich down and wiped my mouth with a napkin, trying to buy myself a little more time. In the end, I decided to just go with the truth. I was a really rotten liar, and Grace knew me so well that I had no chance of getting away with it. "Why is he still here?" I said, answering her question with another question.

"Because he likes you. I know that you're a little out of practice where relationships are concerned, but I figured even you could puzzle that one out."

"He could be married for all we know. It isn't right."

"And where is this imaginary wife of his? It's been a week and there's still no sign of her. Call me crazy, but I think that if someone wanted to find him, he would have been found by now."

"Maybe there was a car accident."

"A car accident," she repeated skeptically.

"Yes! That would explain everything. Ben and his wife were in an accident, and he lost his memory!"

"And walked away without a scratch? In his bathrobe?"

"It's a plausible explanation."

"There are several plausible explanations, but I hardly think that's the most likely one."

"She could be in a hospital somewhere, in a coma. I'd like to think that if my husband was running around with no memory while I was lying helpless in Intensive Care that all those predatory single girls out there would show a little compassion."

"Whatever. At this rate, you'll never have to worry about that scenario. You'd have to find a husband first."

"Grace! That's so mean!"

"It's not mean, it's honest. If someone was coming forward to claim Ben, it would have happened already, coma or not. What are you waiting for?"

"I'm waiting to see if he has a reason to go."

"Well, in the meantime, why don't you try giving him a reason to *stay*?"

"I wish it were that easy."

"It could be if you'd stop overcomplicating it!"

I hesitated. I really wasn't ready to be having this conversation, not even with Grace. "I know that you're only trying to do what's best for me, but you're just going to have to trust me on this one. Things can't go any further with Ben until I'm absolutely sure."

"Sure about what? Who he is and where he came from? And what if that never happens? What if Ben *never* gets his memory back? Are you really going to let him go on the off chance that a hypothetical someone might show up somewhere down the road?"

"I don't know yet."

"Fine, then. I'll make it easy for you. I've got a friend I want to set him up with. I'm going to ask him about it when he gets here." Her voice had an air of finality that made my stomach plunge.

"No," I said quickly.

"Why not? If you don't want him, what do you care who he dates?"

I agonized over what to tell her, how to explain, but I couldn't.

"That's what I thought. I think that the time has come for you to take decisive action."

The door opened, saving me from having to hear exactly what "decisive action" entailed.

"Grace, I'm hurt," Ben said, his arms full of bags.

"Why?"

"The minute I turn my back, you show up with food."

The anxious expression on her face relaxed. "Don't worry; I brought you some sandwiches too." She pushed the bag across the table to where Ben was standing. He peeked in the bag, giving her one of his most charming smiles.

"You have unexpected depths. It's clear that Abbie isn't the only one who's gifted in the food arena."

She blushed. "It's just chicken salad."

"Well, it looks delicious. Thank you, Grace."

"You're welcome. I'm afraid I have to get going. I've got a neighbor who agreed to watch the kids for a minute, and I don't want to take advantage of her." She paused, her hand on the door. "By the way, Ben . . . have you remembered anything?"

I shot her a warning look, but she simply smiled innocently at Ben.

He shook his head. "I'm afraid not."

"And I guess there haven't been any other leads on your identity?"

"Not yet."

"It's hard to believe the police haven't made any progress yet. That must be so frustrating . . . for *both* of you," she said, emphasizing the last part.

My eyes widened at the implications of her remark. "Thanks for lunch, Grace," I said. "We don't want to keep you." I opened the door for her, giving her an outraged look that I hoped communicated how much trouble she was in.

She ignored my look, leaned in, and gave me an impulsive hug. "Be brave—go for it!" she hissed in my ear. I groaned and pushed her out the door.

"So, I guess I don't have to ask what the lunchtime conversation consisted of," Ben said wryly.

"I love Grace, but honestly, she can be completely insensitive sometimes. I'm sorry."

"No harm done."

"Did you find everything on the list?" I said, trying to get away from the topic.

"Yup." He dumped the bags he was carrying on the counter.

"I really owe you for doing this. I don't know if I could have finished it all by myself."

"I'm just glad I could help. What else can I do?"

"Eat your sandwiches."

He grinned. "Yes, ma'am."

"Grace really likes you."

Ben gave me a meaningful look. "Yeah, too bad she's already taken."

I picked up a dishtowel and threw it at him, and he put his hands up defensively.

"I'm *kidding*!"

That night and the next morning passed quickly in a whirl

of last minute preparations—the decorations, the food, and all the other things that were necessary for a knockout New Year's Eve party. Ben even set up a television in the lobby so that everyone could have a front row seat for the official beginning of the year.

Night fell, and at 9:00, people started to arrive. The stage was set.

✳ ✳ ✳ ✳ ✳ ✳ ✳

"This is a great party, sis. You've really outdone yourself this year," Jack commented.

"Well, thank you, Jack." I was frankly surprised that he'd noticed. "I couldn't have done it without Ben, especially not with this temporarily useless foot of mine." I was still saddled with the boot, but I'd abandoned my crutches for the night. My foot was feeling good enough to walk on it without them.

"I suppose. On the other hand, if it weren't for Ben, you wouldn't have been all crippled in the first place," Jack pointed out.

"Jack! This was not his fault."

"No, he's right," Ben said, suddenly appearing behind me. "If it weren't for me, you wouldn't be hobbling around in pain. I still feel really bad for making you go sledding."

"I'm a big girl. I could have said no."

"Isn't peer pressure such a tragedy?" Ben said, shaking his head.

Grace and Jack both laughed, and I couldn't help smiling myself. "In the future, I'll try to remember to just say no to winter sports. Can I get anyone anything?"

"Everything is perfect," Ben assured me. "Why don't you try to just relax and enjoy the evening?"

"He doesn't know you very well, does he?" Grace chimed in.

"I'll just go check to make sure we aren't running low

on anything," I said, ignoring her jab about my OCD inner hostess. I walked across the room to where the serving table was, noting that we were almost out of cream puffs. I visited with a few people I hadn't seen in a while before retrieving the platter to refill. As I turned, Ben was still standing with Grace and Jack and the kids, looking very much like he belonged. Morgan handed him a cookie and he took it, kissing her hand. This gesture caused two bright spots of color to appear in her cheeks. She was smitten, and who could blame her? I suddenly found myself feeling jealous of Morgan, with her uncomplicated, little girl crush. I longed for those bygone simple days, when my head and my heart weren't at war with each other.

Ben looked in my direction, his eyes locking with mine across the room, burning a trail from where he stood to my unsteady heart. It beat nervously, faster and faster, until I was afraid I might suffer some actual physical harm. I wondered if anyone had ever died like this, their heart driven into massive overload due to a mere look. It seemed like such a love struck teenager thing to consider, and I chalked it up to the lateness of the hour. I smiled uneasily at Ben before retreating into the kitchen to collect my thoughts.

I made myself busy adding more cream puffs to the depleted tray. I suspected that there was no way Ben would just leave it at that, but I needed a minute to compose myself before seeing him again, and my hostess duties seemed like a good excuse. My fingers were grateful for a mundane task to complete. Perhaps it might even help to cool the fire that cropped up every time his brown eyes lingered on mine.

"Abbie?" I heard a familiar but tentative voice in the doorway.

My heart undid all its good work, immediately clocking in at full speed again. "Yes?" I replied without turning around. My voice was shaky, but I prayed that Ben couldn't tell. I could hear his casual footsteps approaching until he was hovering at my back.

"It's almost time; you're going to miss it," he chided, his

breath on my neck driving me to distraction.

"We were out of cream puffs," I said as matter-of-factly as I could under the circumstances. His hands moved to my arms, and I tried to swallow my involuntary gasp.

"I don't think anyone really noticed," he said, his voice soft.

I tried to concentrate on straightening the cream puffs, sprinkling them evenly with powdered sugar while inwardly, my heart turned cartwheels. I could hear people beginning to chant in the other room as they began the countdown.

"Ten . . . nine . . . eight . . . seven . . ."

Ben's hands were on my shoulders now, and he slowly swiveled me around so that I was facing him instead of the counter. I kept my eyes down, afraid to meet his, afraid of what I might see.

"Six . . . five . . . four . . ."

He lifted my chin until I was forced to look into his face. His eyes were sparkling, yet contained an urgency that was unmistakable. He slowly leaned in a bit closer, so slowly that I knew he was giving me the opportunity to break away if I wasn't interested. He finally rested his forehead against mine, still giving me the chance to stop him if I wanted to, but I was frozen. I could feel his chest rising and falling against mine, and I'd never been more scared in my life. At the same time, I'd never wanted anything more. My heart thumped so fast now that I wasn't sure I could slow it, even if my life depended on it.

"Three . . . two . . . one . . ."

I knew there was no turning back, and I didn't want to. I simply allowed my eyes to drift closed and surrendered to the situation. Ben brushed his lips gently against mine several times, the barest whisper of a kiss.

"Happy New Year!" the raucous voices proclaimed from afar, barely registering in my clouded brain and ringing ears.

Ben pulled away reluctantly, searching my face to see how I would react. I closed the space between us, grabbed his face with both hands, and pressed my lips against his much more firmly than he'd dared. He wrapped me in his arms and squeezed me until I felt giddy and lightheaded. I was so caught up in his embrace that I didn't hear the footsteps until it was too late. A sharp squeak of surprise came from the doorway, and I immediately disentangled myself, red-faced and embarrassed, to discover Grace cowering, her eyes fixed on the floor.

"I am *so* sorry," she stammered, fleeing at top speed back into the lobby.

Ben looked slightly sheepish but overwhelmingly smug. He gave me a lopsided grin, but I couldn't bring myself to return it.

"That should *not* have happened," I said sternly.

His smile faded abruptly. "Abbie—"

"No, that was wrong." I drew in a shaky breath. "I got caught up in the moment, but I never should have kissed you."

"Actually, I believe it was the other way around. I kissed you," he said, moving toward me in such a way that I was afraid he might try it again.

"Stop!" I warned, using my hands as a barrier. "I kissed you too, if you remember."

"Yes, I noticed that," he said, amusement evident in his tone. "But I kissed you first."

"It was a mistake," I said, trying to make my voice as firm as I knew it should be.

He snorted. "It was a miracle! Why are you resisting this?"

"Because!" I said, waving my arms around like a flustered lunatic.

"Because is not a reason."

I glowered at him. "You know exactly why."

"Look, I know that you think there's a chance I might belong to someone else, but—"

"Enough," I said abruptly, cutting him off. "We've done this bit, over and over. It seems we are at an impasse, and now is not the time to hash it out. Everyone will be leaving, and I need to say good-bye."

"Do what you have to do. I'll wait," he said with a lazy grin, as if he had all the time in the world.

The fact that he wasn't even rumpled by my rebuff made me even more frazzled. I stomped off into the lobby where the party was beginning to break up. I noticed that Grace, Jack and the kids were conspicuously absent. Grace must have rounded them up and run away before she could interrupt my supposed tryst any further.

I smiled and joked, wanting to make sure everyone had had a great time until finally I closed the door behind the last guest. I lingered with my hand on the doorknob, wishing desperately that there was some straggler who had stuck around, not wanting the evening to end. There's always one or two you have to practically throw out—where were they when you actually needed them? I would have been willing to chat about the most mundane subject into the wee hours, anything to keep me from having to face Ben again.

I sighed. He obviously wasn't going anywhere. Whether I was ready or not, there was no use in prolonging the inevitable. I braced myself and went back to the kitchen, poking my head around the corner furtively. Ben was sitting at the bar, his head resting on the counter. His face was peaceful, his eyes closed. It reminded me of the first time I saw him under my Christmas tree. I couldn't believe it was only a week ago that I met him. How had we gotten so close in such a short time?

I watched Ben for a minute, his breathing regular and even, and my heart softened a little thinking about how he'd fallen asleep waiting for me. I put my hand on his shoulder, shaking it gently. "Wake up, Sleeping Beauty. The party's over, and it's time to go home."

His eyes were bleary, and he rubbed them with the back of his hand, momentarily disoriented. "Man, I can't believe I fell asleep. What terrible manners I have."

"It's okay. It is pretty late."

He yawned. "What time is it?"

"Just after one."

He made an attempt to shake off sleep and look alert. "Let's get this place cleaned up."

"Tomorrow," I said.

"But—"

"I'm closed on New Year's Day. There will be plenty of time to clean then. Come on, I'll drive you home."

He gave in. I put my coat on, took his arm, and led him through the door and toward the car. A sudden breeze made it seem a lot chillier than I had expected, and Ben rubbed his arms in an attempt to get warm.

"Where's your coat?" I scolded.

"I must have left it inside."

I slid the key to the bakery off the ring and tossed the other keys to Ben. "You start the car, and I'll get it." He was too sleepy to argue.

Ben's coat was on the coat rack, right where it should be. I grabbed it and headed for the door.

It beeped at me.

The noise would have been hard to detect in a crowded room, but in the empty bakery, it was startling. Maybe sleep deprivation was causing me to imagine things; coats don't generally beep. I gingerly patted down the pockets, freezing when I felt something square-ish and solid. I knew that I shouldn't be doing this. What business of mine was it what Ben carried in his pockets?

I knew it was a complete invasion of his privacy, but I couldn't help myself. I reached into his pocket with my eyes squeezed shut tight, as if I might touch a poisonous snake.

It was a Blackberry—a very normal thing to find in anyone's pocket, except Ben's. Where did he get it, and why would a guy with amnesia need a Blackberry? I told myself that maybe he'd wanted the police station to be able to reach him at any hour.

1 new message

This had disaster written all over it, but it was too late to turn back now.

I opened the message, scanning it quickly as a frosty wave barreled through my body, flash freezing everything and rendering me almost instantly numb. Although I was appreciative of my body's protective gesture on my behalf, it came a second too late to prevent the sharp stab of pain that slipped through. I read it again in shock.

"Why is your face on the news, John Doe? Why haven't you told her who you really are? Did something go wrong?"

Thirteen

* * * * * * * * * * *

I opened the car door and threw Ben's coat at him. He looked surprised but said nothing. "Oh, and you have a message," I said tartly.

He was completely awake now, and he suddenly looked a little pale. "What kind of message?" he said, his tone neutral.

"I think you know. Go on, check it—it might be important."

Ben reluctantly reached into his coat pocket and pulled out his Blackberry. He read the message quickly. If he seemed uneasy before, he looked positively ill now. "Abbie, I can explain—"

"Can you?" Something inside me snapped. I hit him in the chest with my fist, and then continued to pummel him with both hands, not hard enough to cause any real damage, but still sharp enough to let him know I wasn't kidding around. He just sat there, waiting for me to exhaust my rage. "How could you, Ben?" I yelled.

"If you'll just listen—"

"Oh, I'm sorry; it isn't really Ben, is it? What's your *real* name?"

"I tried to tell you."

"You must not have tried very hard because I think I would have remembered that."

"I tried to tell you after dinner on Sunday. I tried to tell you after we kissed tonight—"

"I don't think you should mention that right now," I said dangerously. "I feel like enough of a fool already without you rubbing my face in it."

"You're overreacting. This isn't really as bad as it seems. Once I explain it to you, you'll see."

"I'm through playing this game with you. I want to know who you are. *Right now.*"

A ghost of a smile crossed Ben's features. "You sounded exactly like my mother just then."

I gave him a short, terse laugh. "All of the sudden, you have a mother! Forgive me for not congratulating you. Is this some sort of scam?" I demanded.

"No," he said wearily.

"Then tell me what's going on. I don't appreciate being lied to."

"I couldn't tell you who I was right away because you never would have believed me."

I folded my arms across my chest. "Well, now's your big chance, so start talking."

Ben took a deep breath. "Santa really did put me under your tree, but not in the way you think."

My eyes widened. "You've *got* to be kidding me. *This* is your story?" I said.

"Are you going to let me finish or not?"

"Knock yourself out."

"I met Santa a few years ago—"

"I don't mean to interrupt, but I'm curious—how does one get to be on a first name basis with Santa Claus?"

"I told you, I met him. I was doing a piece on this extreme marathon they have in the North Pole. The travel magazine I write for thought it would be a great story if I went there and participated in it."

"So, you're a writer . . . and a runner."

"Well, I'm not much of a runner, but yes."

"Do they really have a marathon in the North Pole?"

"Yeah, it's crazy. They fly you in there by helicopter, and you run on ice that's only a few feet above the ocean. It's like a challenge for people who aren't satisfied with completing a regular marathon. I'm glad I got to do it—with global warming, there probably won't be ice at the North Pole in a few years."

"So you enjoyed yourself?"

"It was terrible! I kept looking around thinking, who are these people, anyway? They were machines! And then there was me, exhausted and shivering—like running twenty-six miles in a normal climate isn't bad enough."

"And while you were there, you just happened to run into Santa," I said dubiously.

"Something like that."

"Did you put *that* in your article?"

"What do you think?"

"You know, most rational adults are of the school that says Santa Claus doesn't exist." I felt like a little girl again with one of my uncles pulling my leg, waiting to see if I would fall for it. I usually did—I was notoriously gullible.

"Have you ever been to the North Pole?"

"Of course not," I stammered.

"Then you'll just have to take my word for it. Since then, Santa and I have become quite good friends. We hit it off right away—we have the same initials, you know."

I thought back to the monogrammed pajamas. "SBC?"

"Sterling Benjamin Carlisle."

"You don't really expect me to believe that your middle name is actually Ben, do you?"

"I was surprised when you said it, but it's a fairly common name. And if you ever tell Santa that I told you his middle name is Beauregard, I'll deny it."

"So you and Santa just hung out together."

"Even Santa doesn't work 24/7. He needs a little downtime too. We went fishing—ice fishing, of course. I caught one that was *this big*!" he said, holding his hands apart about three feet.

I gave him the tiniest of smiles, despite my simmering anger. "Don't mix fish stories with fables."

"Anyway, Santa called me a couple of days before Christmas. He told me he felt bad because a very good girl wasn't going to get what she asked for. He was afraid she would be really disappointed on Christmas morning. I told him that he'd always been able to pull off impossible requests before, so why should this be any different? He said that there was no way he could give her what she asked for . . . but that I might. I couldn't imagine what I might give someone that he couldn't. So he showed me your letter."

"Wait a minute. There's no way he could have showed you my letter because I didn't write it until Christmas Eve."

Ben looked puzzled. "I've got it right here in my pocket." He unfolded it and handed it across to me.

"Dear Santa," I read aloud. "What I would really like for Christmas is a man. I know it's a lot to ask for, but I've been *really* good this year. Love, Abbie." I shrugged. "I didn't write this. It looks like someone emailed it . . ." Suddenly it was glaringly obvious. "Grace!" I growled angrily. "Why can't she just mind her own business?"

"But she said she didn't do it."

"Yeah, well, she said she didn't take my Malibu Beach Barbie when we were kids, but guess what I found hiding under her pillow?" I muttered. Ben gave me a strange look. "Grace told me that her kids went to this website to send their letters to Santa this year. She must have included a little request of her own on my behalf. I never imagined that they went directly to the man himself."

"Actually, Santa never sees most of the letters. The elves only give him the really tricky ones."

"The elves?" I echoed.

Ben sighed. "You know . . . the elves who work in Santa's workshop?"

I shook my head. "Never mind. So, Santa showed you the letter—"

"He emailed it to me, actually."

I ignored him. " . . . and you automatically agreed to be my present?"

"Not exactly. I was . . . hesitant."

"I can understand why. It's a little bit crazy."

"It's not even that. It's just, well, there's a reason I live alone. I haven't dated for a long time. I travel a lot for work and that keeps me pretty busy. Plus, I was tired of all the games."

"That's rich," I scoffed. "If this isn't a game, I don't know what is."

"This was necessary. If I'd told you on Christmas morning what I just told you now, you'd have had me committed. I needed a little time to get to know you first."

"But if you were tired of dating, then why did you agree to do this in the first place?"

"Your letter was so simple and honest. I could tell that you were lonely, and I was lonely, and I'm not exactly getting any younger. So I thought what have you got to lose by just meeting her? Plus, it's really hard to turn Santa down. And I had a contingency plan, in case it didn't work out."

"You mean, in case I had sixteen cats and spent all my free time knitting little sweaters for them?"

"That was a concern, yes," he replied, smiling. "My boss, Leon, was the only person who knew I was going to do this, besides Santa, of course. He was the one who sent me the message just now. He arranged for a courier to drop off my Blackberry once I got a hotel room. If I sent him a certain message, he would have someone show up, claiming to be my wife."

My mouth dropped open. "Veronica!"

"No, no—that was a complete coincidence," he assured me. "There was no reason to call in the cavalry because I was having a good time with you."

"What was your emergency exit message?"

He grinned widely. "Houston, we have a problem."

I rolled my eyes. "I feel like I'm in some secret agent movie. What about you showing up at church? You seemed to be awfully familiar with the whole process."

"I am a member of the Church, if that's what you're asking, but I haven't been active for a few years. It was easy to let myself get out of the habit of going to meetings because of all of the traveling I was doing for work, and after a while I didn't go even when I had the chance because I felt so guilty. I meant what I said about it feeling like coming home. You don't realize what you're missing until you go back after being away. It made me think that maybe it's time to get my priorities in order."

I didn't know what to say. Everything seemed to be falling neatly into place, but I couldn't come to terms with the fact that he'd deliberately kept me in the dark about everything that was important to him.

I was silent for a minute, thinking. "So, you agree to fill my request; then what happened?"

"I flew out . . ."

"In the sleigh?" I said incredulously.

Ben laughed. "No, on a plane.

"Did you wear your pajamas on the flight?"

"Not exactly. I changed in the airport when I arrived, and I took a cab to your house."

"Didn't the cab driver think your attire was a little odd?"

"He did give me a funny look, but I imagine he's seen stranger things. Plus, I gave him a really big tip."

"But why go to all that trouble? You could have just worn normal clothes."

"I was hoping that if I was wearing pajamas, it might buy me some time and throw everyone off the trail. A guy in his pajamas can only get so far without being noticed, so I thought that might convince everyone to keep the search local, at least for a while."

"And how did you get into my house?"

"Luckily, the door was unlocked."

"I've really *got* to stop doing that."

"I know; anyone could walk in." When I didn't stop him, he continued. "I sat in the chair in your living room until I got sleepy. I kept dozing off until I actually fell out of it."

"That must have been the thump that woke me up."

"And suddenly, there you were, wielding your trusty rolling pin. I must say, I liked you from the beginning."

"Then why weren't you honest with me?"

"I told you, we needed time to get to know each other."

I shook my head dismissively. "I'm not buying it. What happened to my real letter?"

"I took it."

"Didn't you think it was odd that there was a different letter by the tree?"

"I just thought you were very thorough."

"What about the Coke and the Pringles?'

"I ate them. It was a long flight—I was hungry."

"This isn't funny. You lied to me . . . a lot. How can I trust what you're saying now?"

"Abbie, sometimes you just have to take a leap of faith."

"I don't do leaping anymore. When I leap, people leave."

"I'm not going anywhere."

"Yes, you are."

He looked confused.

"You're going back to the hotel while I decide what to do." I started the car, and we drove the short distance in silence.

"Couldn't we talk about this?" Ben said finally.

I put the car in park, but I didn't bother turning off the engine. "It's late, and besides, we've done the talking."

"I've come a long way to meet you—"

I put up one hand to stop him talking. "Assuming that I believe your crazy story, which is a lot to accept, I need some time to decide."

"Decide what?"

"Whether I can ever believe anything you say again. You let me think you had no memory, and I agonized over whether or not you were already taken. You lied to me. How can I get past that?"

"The only thing I pretended was that I didn't know who

I was. Everything else was real, I swear." Ben put his hand on my arm, searching my eyes for signs I might give in. "I really like you, more than anyone in a long time. When I kissed you, I thought I could tell that you liked me too."

I smiled sadly. "I don't know if that's enough."

✳ ✳✳✳✳✳ ✳

"You did *not* say that. Abbie, he's perfect."

Of course Grace would take his side. Hypothetically, she could probably find out that Ben killed somebody, and she would forgive him because at least it was only one person. "He lied. He's a liar! Why can no one understand that?"

"But he had a good reason! Admit it—if he told you that Santa sent him the minute you laid eyes on him, you would have called the police."

"Wouldn't you?"

"Well, yes. But now . . . ?"

"I don't know!"

Grace was helping me clean up the bakery on New Year's Day. We'd finished taking down the decorations and had moved on to the giant stack of dishes in the kitchen. The kids were playing Monopoly in the lobby. Ben had not made an appearance, and I doubted that he would. I was pretty sure that he would wait for me to make the first move, and while I appreciated the space, my sister certainly wasn't making my decision any easier. I knew that when she offered to come over and clean that she was really just looking for juicy details, and I got the distinct impression that her help would come at a very steep price.

"Why did you do it, anyway?" I said finally.

"Send the letter?"

I nodded.

"I told you, I didn't send it."

"Right. The cat's out of the bag now, so you might as well admit it. I've heard that confession is good for the soul."

"I'm telling you the truth, Abbie. I didn't send the letter. I only wish I could take credit for it."

I put my hands on my hips. "Who else would do something like this but you?"

"Look, I admit it seems suspicious, but it really wasn't me. I imagine that whoever sent it knew you'd never ask yourself. I don't know anyone who deserves to have someone in their life as much as you do. But you've given up."

"I haven't given up," I bristled. "My life is just fine the way it is. I'm very happy."

"Are you?"

I didn't answer because there were tears in the corners of my eyes and I didn't trust myself to speak.

"Someone went to a lot of trouble to get this guy here, so give him a chance, okay?"

I gave Grace a big hug, which was tricky since her hands were still buried almost to the elbow in the dishwater. My tears fell easily now. There was a tentative rapping at the door in the other room. I grabbed a tissue and dabbed at my eyes.

"I can get it," Grace offered, taking her hands out of the soapy water to grab a dishtowel.

"No, you're all wet. I'm okay."

I went out into the lobby, where Jake was already trying to unlock the door. "Someone's here."

"I heard, but you shouldn't open the door until you know who it is. Honestly, can't people read a sign?" I mumbled under my breath.

"It could be a stranger," Hannah said ominously.

I froze when I got to the door and saw those familiar brown eyes staring back at me through the glass.

Jake stood on his tiptoes but still wasn't tall enough to see out. "Well? Is it a stranger?"

"He's a little strange," I said in a distracted tone. I opened the door.

"Hello."

"Hi."

He noticed my red eyes. "Is everything okay?"

"Grace and I were just having a talk."

"If I came at a bad time, I can go."

"Everything is fine," I said, leaning against the doorframe.

"So . . . can I come in?"

"We're closed," I said, ever the master of stating the obvious.

"I didn't exactly come for cake."

I was being silly. "Of course, come in."

Jake was thrilled when he saw who it was. "Ben!" he said happily, holding his closed fist out for Ben. Ben smiled, bumping his own knuckles against Jake's in greeting. Seeing how well they got along made my heart ache a little.

"Hello, Ben," Morgan said shyly. "We're playing Monopoly. Do you want to play?"

"I'd love to, but I'm afraid I'm already spoken for. I'm here to help clean up."

Grace peered around the corner. "Abbie, I'm sorry, but we really have to get home. Oh, hello, Ben."

"Well hello, Grace."

"That was some party last night, wasn't it?" she said.

"Definitely one for the books."

"Come on kids, we've got to go."

"But we're right in the middle of a game!" Jake protested. "And I'm winning."

"You can start over when we get home. I hate to leave you with the rest of this mess, but Hannah has a piano lesson this afternoon."

"Don't worry about it. You already helped me a lot," I assured her.

When the kids made no immediate move to pick up the game, Grace picked up the board and folded it into the box. Jake groaned. "Mom, you're mixing up all the money!"

Grace handed him the box. "Maybe next time you'll pick it up on your own when I tell you to, hmmm?"

Hannah looked confused. "I thought my lesson was cancelled this week."

"Why would you think that, sweetie?"

"Because you said—"

"Oh, look at the time. It's even later than I thought. Good to see you, Ben."

"Maybe you can come over and play Monopoly with us later, huh, Ben?" Jake said.

Ben looked at me, searching for some idea of what to tell him. "I hope so."

I glared at Grace as she dragged the kids outside. I knew she'd invented an excuse so I would be left alone with Ben.

"Not winning any awards for subtlety, your sister, but I still like her." Ben pulled up a chair and sat down, patting the one next to him. I sat in it reluctantly.

"I didn't think I'd see you here today."

"I did promise I'd help you clean up."

"Yes, but that was before . . ."

"Right. I was clinging to this small hope that I'd dreamed the last part of the evening and that when I got here, everything would still be okay."

"I'm sorry. I'm just really confused right now."

"Couldn't we start over? I'll even go out and come in again if you want. I'll be myself right from the beginning."

"It's not that easy."

"Maybe you're making it harder than it needs to be."

"Can't you see I'm doing my best?"

"What—to chase me away? You're doing a pretty good job."

"No! Yes! I've been trying my hardest not to care about you."

"Why?"

"I told you why. Because I didn't want to fall apart when your wife and six kids showed up and whisked you away."

"And I understand that. But why are you pushing me away now?"

"Because you lied to me."

"Abbie, I want you to listen to me very carefully. I did what I did because it was the only way I could see for us to get to know each other that didn't end with me in a straightjacket. It may have been right, and it may have been wrong—either way, it's done. I can't go back and change it, and I don't even know if I would. I feel like I was given a rare opportunity and, other than the fact that I had to deceive you, I think it all turned out very well. So, I guess what you have to ask yourself is do you like me enough to give me the benefit of the doubt? Are you invested enough to take that leap and see what happens?"

"I like you a lot, Ben," I started.

"But . . . ?"

"I got to a point in my life where I told myself that I was done putting my heart through the wringer, and I meant it."

He clenched his jaw in frustration. "You are the most stubborn person I've ever met. You're determined not to let me in simply because you've already decided that there is no one out there for you, and admitting that you have feelings for me would crush the plan that you've so carefully laid out for yourself."

"I am determined not to get hurt again, if that's what you mean. And you've already misled me once."

"Okay, then help me understand. If you didn't want a relationship, why did you ask for one?"

I shrugged, one tear escaping and making a track down my cheek before I could stop it. "It was safe. I knew that I took no risk in asking for it because no one would ever know but me." I wiped my eyes, trying not to look at Ben. I was surprised to discover just how much I feared disappointing him. But after all this time living with my feelings turned off, I was afraid it would be too overwhelming to try to resurrect them now. "I want to trust you, but it's just too scary. I'm sorry."

"Yeah, me too," he said, his voice hollow.

We both sat there for a minute, letting the last words wash over us until they settled. Ben finally stood, and I guessed that meant he was leaving, so I stood too. I awkwardly offered him my hand to shake. "Good-bye, Ben," I said.

He took my hand, using it to pull me into his arms instead. He held me so tight, his fingers digging into my skin as if that could keep me from slipping away. "Are you sure about this?" he asked softly, his warm breath tickling my ear. I shivered, closing my eyes. Was this really happening? My brain felt slow and everything around me was happening too fast. I knew I couldn't honestly tell Ben that all was forgiven, but was I really ready to let him go? As much as I wanted this thing with Ben to be real, I kept coming back to the sad truth that our whole relationship was built on a fantasy. I didn't know if I could survive if I jumped in and it crumbled around me.

"I want to, but I just can't."

He pulled away, his eyes full of hurt. "You can tell yourself whatever you want if it makes you feel better, but I know the truth. It's not really me you don't trust—it's yourself. You've put your heart under lock and key, and you're afraid that if you tried to use it now, it wouldn't know how to function. But hearts are like riding bicycles, Abbie; you never really forget." He dropped my hand, and it was only then that I realized he'd been holding it all along.

Ben walked to the door, stopping with his hand on the knob. "I'm going home, to New York. It's a big place, but not impossible to find someone if you wanted to."

I turned to face him. "I'm really sorry you came all this way for nothing."

"Not as sorry as I am, I guess. Take care of yourself, Abbie." Ben plunged through the door before I could reply.

I took a deep breath, letting it out slowly. I told myself that I felt nothing but relief. I'd made my decision years ago—no more guys, no more heartache. Up until now, it had served me well. I decided that I was wrong to let Grace talk me into asking Santa for a man because I was doing just fine on my own. That empty feeling in my chest was only a temporary condition; everything would be okay now. After all, Ben couldn't very well leave me if I left him first.

Fourteen

* * * * * * * *

I finished the rest of the cleaning on autopilot, locking up and going home as soon as I was finished. I wandered from room to room, straightening pillows and picture frames. I turned on the television, flipping through all the channels idly several times, but I found that I couldn't concentrate on anything, and I couldn't sit still. My phone rang a couple of times, and part of me hoped that it would be Ben, but it was just Grace. I let it ring. I hoped to put off that particular conversation as long as possible.

It seemed absurd to be thinking about going to bed at 6:00, but at the same time, it hardly seemed worth aimlessly rattling around the house for another couple of hours. I put on my pajamas and crawled under the covers, hoping that sleep would clear my head. It seemed like an eternity before I finally dozed off.

When my alarm rang, I seriously considered just unplugging it and taking up permanent residence in my bed. But I forced myself to get up and go in to work. It was silly to just sit at home, moping. And this was what I wanted, right? For things to go back to the way they were before? Yes, work was exactly what I needed right now. I'd always been able to lose myself in baking, no matter what else was happening in my life. It was my great escape, and I knew that getting back into that routine as soon as possible would help me feel normal.

The morning was going as well as could be expected until I went into the kitchen to grab something to eat before I left. When I opened my cupboard crowded with cereal boxes, I heard Ben's voice teasing me. I tried to swallow a couple of bites of Lucky Charms but couldn't seem to get them past the lump that suddenly appeared in my throat. I dumped them down the sink and left, determined to get to work. My foot actually felt pretty good this morning. Once I got started cooking, everything else would just fall into place.

I half expected Ben to be waiting by the door when I arrived, and I told myself that I was relieved when he wasn't, despite my traitor heart and its annoying flip-flops of disappointment. Although his leaving was abrupt, it was undoubtedly better this way. No reason to draw out the inevitable. I started flipping through cookbooks, looking for something complicated to occupy my brain. As I was turning the pages, I stumbled onto a piece of paper with unfamiliar handwriting. My heart throbbed dully as I recognized what it was—Ben's oatmeal raisin cookie recipe.

My eyes blurred with tears, making it almost impossible for me to make out the writing. I used the corner of my apron to blot them away, and the page jumped into focus. "Mix 25 big spoons of oatmeal with four handfuls of raisins," it began, and under this instruction it said, "(Maybe six handfuls of raisins for you—my hands are a lot bigger than yours.)"

I couldn't bring myself to read the rest of it except for the small personal note at the bottom, where my eyes drifted without my permission. "Abbie, I know that this recipe is outside the realm of your comfort zone, but if you keep an open mind, I know you can make it work. Ben."

I shook my head, sending the tears racing down my cheeks. Why, out of all the cookbooks I could have picked up did I have to choose that one today? If I had found this small memento years or even months down the road, it would have been bittersweet, but not fatal. Now it was like I could barely breathe. The room was getting smaller, and my chest was getting tighter. Maybe I was having a heart attack. That really would be the final irony. Just when I'd discovered a use for it too, poor thing. It had sat idle but content in my chest for years, and now I'd gone and wrecked it unnecessarily.

I sat in a chair and took some deep breaths after hiding the recipe in a book I barely ever used. I told myself that maybe by the time I stumbled onto it again, it wouldn't hurt so much. The little voice in my head questioned whether I'd recently developed masochistic tendencies, and if I hadn't, why I'd chosen to suffer when I didn't have to.

Ben could be here right now if you hadn't chickened out and chased him away, it scolded.

Yes, but what about the lies? I shot back.

Lie, it corrected. *There was only one.*

Only one that we knew about, and it was a really big one, I argued. *How could I ever trust him again? I would always be wondering what else he might be hiding.*

He really cares about you. Think of all the people out there, searching for what you're wasting. Why can't you just give him a break?

It's too late now. He's already gone.

So, get him back!

I pushed the voice away. I was sick of listening to it, probably because it was right. I heard the doorbell in the lobby, and it filled me with dread. There was no way I could do this today. Cooking probably would help me to relax, but I'd forgotten that I would have to see people too. Whoever it was, I would just have to apologize and send them on their way. I would go back home and do whatever I had to do to get myself together for tomorrow.

"Hey, sis. You in there?" Jack's voice carried through from the entry.

I cleared my throat. "Yeah, I'll be right out." What was Jack doing here? This was all I needed right now; he would tell Grace for sure. I dried my face and put on the happiest expression I could manage. I peeked around the corner. He was staring, puzzled, into the empty glass case.

"I hate to rush you, but I'm kind of in a hurry. I've got an early meeting this morning, and I told them I'd bring the goodies. I figured you wouldn't mind a little free advertising."

I stepped into the lobby. "It was nice of you to think of me, Jack. I'm sorry to disappoint you, but there aren't any goodies this morning," I said.

Jack studied me for a minute, trying to decide what the best approach was. Apparently, he came to the conclusion that there was no way for him to escape without making inquiries, however painful that might be. "You look terrible," he finally blurted out. "Did something happen?"

"Everything is fine. I just got a late start this morning," I said evenly. "I wish I had something to give you, but there aren't even any leftovers."

"Don't worry about it." He looked longingly at the door, but stayed rooted to the spot. I could see the wheels spinning in his head, and I knew he was kicking himself, thinking about how much easier it would have been to stop by the grocery store for doughnuts, where there were no crying women to contend with.

"You'd better go. Don't want to be late for your meeting," I said, giving him permission to flee.

"Right." He looked relieved as he headed for the exit, but turned and made one last-ditch effort. "I know I'm not exactly Grace, but if there was something you wanted to talk about—"

"Grace is precisely the last person I want to talk to right now."

"Why? You've obviously been crying, and that seems like very girlie territory."

"You wouldn't understand."

"Try me."

"You've got a meeting to get to."

He shrugged. "I didn't want to go anyway. I hate early meetings; whatever brownie points I earn by showing up are cancelled out because I can't help falling asleep."

I laughed, but it came out as more of a sob, and once I started, they just spilled out of my chest in rapid succession.

Jack looked alarmed. "Hey, c'mere," he said, opening his arms. I launched myself into them, burying my face in his shoulder. "Why can't you talk to Grace?" he said, patting me awkwardly on the back.

"B-b-because she'll only yell at m-m-me," I hiccupped.

"She loves you. Whatever it is, it can't be that bad."

I pulled away and looked into Jack's face, to gauge his response. "I told Ben it would never work because he lied to me, and he went home . . . to New York . . . where he lives." Each of my pauses was punctuated by a sob.

"Oh. So, you wanted him to go, and he went?"

"It's just b-b-better this way."

"That's not really an answer to the question."

"Yes, I wanted him to go."

"Then why are you crying?"

"I don't know!"

"Are you *sure* you wanted him to go?"

"I just said I did."

"I'm sorry. Grace really is better at things like this."

"Please don't tell her," I begged.

"Abbie, I think she's going to notice eventually. You can't avoid her forever. Trust me—I know."

"I'm just not ready yet. Promise me you won't say anything."

"My lips are sealed. Anyway, you've heard that saying about killing the messenger . . ."

I hugged him again. "Thank you, Jack. I guess I can see why Grace loves you. And you clean up pretty well. I'm sorry I cried all over your nice shirt."

"Hey, what are brother-in-laws for?"

When Jack left, I scrawled a quick sign, announcing that

the bakery was closed due to illness and taped it to the front door. I drove home and got back into bed, relieved that I wouldn't have to face anyone else today.

✻ ✻ ✻ ✻ ✻ ✻ ✻

I woke to a loud knocking on my door. I looked at my alarm clock—12:30 PM. I rolled over, hoping that whoever it was would give up and go away. After a minute, the knocking stopped, and I was just starting to slip back into a dream I'd been having about Ben. He was trying to tell me something, but every time he opened his mouth, something would happen to stop him. Maybe if I could get right back to sleep, I would finally find out what it was he wanted to say. I pictured Ben in my mind, and sleep curled around me again. He smiled, and I smiled and walked closer, until he was standing right next to me. He moved his hand to my cheek, tracing my jaw line from my ear to my chin. As far as dreams go, this was pretty good. He looked into my eyes, opening his mouth to speak.

"Abbie," he started. But his voice wasn't right. It was too high-pitched. In fact, it sounded almost like . . .

"Abbie!" the voice said more urgently.

I opened my eyes to find Grace's face mere inches from mine. She was standing over the bed, shaking me. I jumped, yelling, which made Grace scream too.

So much for not having to see anyone else today, I thought grimly. Or ever finding out what Ben wanted to tell me, for that matter. There was no way I was getting back to sleep now.

"You scared me to death!" I said when I could catch my breath.

"I didn't mean to. Didn't you hear me knocking? I was getting worried."

"Why would you be worried if I didn't answer the door at home during the day? I should be at work."

"I've just come from there. Why are you closed due to ill-ness? Who's sick?"

"Well, me, obviously."

"I thought maybe Ben had come down with something and needed to be nursed back to health."

"Ben is fine."

"Good. He can take care of you."

"I don't need anyone to take care of me. I can get better all by myself."

"You never know—it might be fun."

I sighed. I was going to have to tell her eventually, and although I wanted to put it off, now was probably as good a time as any. "Ben's gone," I said quickly, turning over onto my side so that I wouldn't have to see her expression.

Grace stormed around to the other side of the bed, hands clenched into fists. "What do you mean, gone?"

"I think it's pretty self-explanatory."

"But I don't understand."

"He went home."

"Yes, I get that. *Why* did he go home?"

"Because it obviously wasn't going to work."

"So you *told* him to go."

"It was a mutual decision," I said defensively.

"I'll bet. Sometimes you completely baffle me. Don't you ever want to get married and have a family of your own?"

When Grace said those words, it was like someone punched me in the gut. I threw off the covers and got up, heading for the door.

"Abbie, wait. I didn't mean that the way it sounded."

"It doesn't matter."

"It *does* matter! I know you think this is none of my busi-ness, but you need to put some serious thought into this before you decide," she said, trailing down the hall after me.

"The decision has already been made."

"If this is something you want, you have to try!"

I spun around on her. "Don't you *dare* try to make this my

fault! I never chose to be alone—it just happened."

"You didn't throw away opportunities, but you haven't gone out of your way to seek them either."

"You don't know anything about how hard it's been for me. I don't need this, *especially* from you—you, married with three great kids, living in a beautiful home . . . and skinny! What do you know about disappointment?"

"This isn't about me," she said gently. "If you're happy being single, then I'm happy for you. You're self-sufficient and when you decide you want something, you go after it and you don't quit until you have it, and I *love* that about you. I admire you so much, how you started the bakery from nothing and made it work. So, if that makes you happy, I'm all for it. But if you think you might want a husband, if you want to have kids, somewhere down the line you're going to have to take a chance on someone. And Ben seems like someone worth taking a chance on."

I didn't know what to say. It's one thing to say you want a husband in a silly letter, in the privacy of your own home. But it's quite another to have him actually show up. How could I have known that, not only was someone listening, but they were in a position to take me seriously?

"I'm not saying this because I want to hurt you. I just don't want you to wake up a few years down the road and realize you made a huge mistake. But whatever you decide, I'm on your side."

"I know you're only trying to do what's best for me, but I really just need some time alone right now."

"But we're still friends, right?"

I gave her a weak smile. "The best."

She gave me a hug. "If you want to talk, you know where to find me."

"Where? Out saving the world, one relationship at a time?"

"No, nothing that exciting. I'll be at home, helping Jake make a shoebox diorama of the Civil War."

✳ ✳ ✳ ✳ ✳ ✳ ✳

I cried after Grace left. Again. The little voice in my head remarked that, for someone who had gotten what they wanted, I was surprisingly weepy. I ignored it.

I went back into my bedroom and stood in front of the window, studying a tree. It was a spindly little tree with flakes of bark peeling from the trunk. It caught the sunlight like an amber snake, shedding its skin to reveal the impossible sleekness and vulnerability of the white wood beneath. I wished it were that easy to just peel off your old life like a skin, leaving it behind. If only I could do that with the time I'd spent with Ben.

I pulled the shades before I went back to bed so I couldn't tell that outside, the sun was struggling to shine. It was a beautiful day and the world was moving on without me. People everywhere were having moments, whether they were sad, or scary, or so happy that they thought their hearts might burst with the sheer joy of being alive. Everyone was moving forward, except me. I was coasting along in neutral, eyes straight ahead, never looking around. If I didn't see what was happening, I wouldn't know what I was missing.

I tried to fall asleep, but it was useless. When I closed my eyes, I saw Ben. I got out of bed and dragged myself to the bathroom. I looked at my reflection in the mirror. My face was puffy from my extended crying jag, and I had this splotchy red mark by my left eye. It happened every time I wept or was outside in the cold—some unique part of my genetic makeup that hung around for hours after, marking me. Looking at it now, I suddenly felt this immense sorrow that there would never be anyone who would know me well enough to recognize it.

I would never have a husband who saw this particular genetic eccentricity as endearing, and who would tease me and wonder if our children would have it too. I wouldn't have to go to the trouble of trying to hide the fact that I'd been crying because there would be no one to hide it from. No one would ever know about my inability to keep a plant alive or my irrational fear of geese, or check to make sure I remembered to lock the door. No one would ever know these things about me.

I was too afraid, and not for the reasons I'd fed myself over the years. In the blinding, unflinching reality of the moment, I knew that I wasn't afraid that someone would leave me as much as of what it might mean if they stayed. I had steadfastly protected myself from my own feelings until I could barely remember what it was like to feel.

I splashed some cold water on my face, and my eyes drifted back to the mirror. I took a hard look at myself, for the first time in a long time. Was I really prepared to live without what I was giving up?

Fifteen

The sun was going down, coating the world with a golden glow. I stared out the window of the plane, wishing that we were flying over an ocean. I remembered once when I was younger, being fascinated on a flight by the seemingly endless stretch of water below and how the clouds had appeared to be resting directly on the surface of the water. I had imagined the waves lapping lightly at the puffy edges. It reminded me of a dessert in an old Betty Crocker cookbook from my childhood. The cover had the imprint of a spiral cooktop burned into the stiff binding. In my early days of experimental baking, I'd accidentally laid it across a hot unit, branding it forever. I loved to look at the pictures, and one in particular I found intriguing. They were called floating desserts: fluffy, meringue-type lumps that bobbed in some sort of punch. I never could figure out quite how you were supposed to eat them, and I never attempted to make them. Just as well, I guess, since there probably wouldn't be much call for that sort of dessert in the bakery now. Of course, people might have been glad to have something different, anything to save them from the monotony of the past month's offerings.

Cupcakes. That's what I'd baked for the last month. Granted, there were lots of different kinds of cupcakes, but still. I couldn't help it—when I'm sad, I make cupcakes, and no matter how much I tried to tell myself every morning that I needed to move on, it was all I could manage. I went through the motions of my life in a trance, thinking that people were lucky that I was opening for business at all. But by the time I left to get on the plane to find Ben, I could tell that even my most loyal customers were losing patience. I closed the bakery, leaving a sign on the door that apologized for my inability to function and promised that when I returned, regardless of the outcome of my trip, they could look forward to something other than cupcakes.

"This is crazy," I mumbled under my breath. I must not have said it quite as softly as I thought, because the man sitting in the chair next to me eyed me curiously. I gave him a shy half smile before turning my attention back to the striking sunset outside my window.

"I'm sorry to bother you, ma'am, but I couldn't help noticing you talking to yourself. Are you nervous?" he inquired.

"You have no idea."

He chuckled, and I turned to face him. He was quite handsome, in a cowboy sort of way. He was wearing Wranglers and boots, and his hair was dark, cut very short. His boots were worn, but clean. I noticed a slight drawl in his voice, like he'd almost managed to lose the accent over time, but not completely.

"Are you afraid of flying? It's actually safer than driving, you know."

"Flying doesn't bother me."

"Then why are you so fidgety? If you don't mind me asking."

"I'm on my way to see someone."

"Someone you haven't seen in a long time?" he guessed. Time came out "tahm;" the accent was a little stronger on certain words.

"It seems like a long time, but really it was only a month ago."

"Did you have a falling out?"

"Something like that."

"Family?"

"Not exactly."

"Oh, I see."

"What do you see?"

"It's a man you're going to visit; that's why you're so nervous," he said knowingly. "Take my advice, ma'am, long-distance relationships don't work. Believe me, I've tried."

"We're not in a relationship, not anymore. Maybe we never were."

"I'm sorry. I didn't mean to upset you."

"It's not your fault."

He paused. "So if you're not together anymore, why are going all this way to see him?"

The stewardess came by then with her cart. "Can I get either of you something to drink?"

"Coke, please," I said.

"Fanta, no ice," the cowboy added.

I choked on the laugh I was trying to suppress.

"What?" he demanded.

"Fanta, no ice?" I said incredulously. "I thought you were a tough cowboy."

"Oh, I am," he assured me.

"Well?"

"What's wrong with Fanta?" He took the fizzy orange drink from the stewardess.

"I was just expecting something a little more . . . masculine. It's the kind of thing a little boy would drink." I sipped my Coke.

"Actually, my grandpa always bought me one at the store when I was little."

"Well, when you put it that way, I guess it's kind of sweet."

"So, you were telling me why you're flying thousands of miles to see someone you don't love."

"I didn't say I don't love him."

"Oh. So you *do* love him?"

"I didn't say that either." I paused, considering my words carefully. "I think I may have made a mistake."

"You think?"

I shrugged helplessly. "I'm still not sure what the right choice is, but I owe it to him to give him a chance. He went to a lot of trouble for me, and I never really appreciated that until he was gone."

"Well, he must be a great guy."

"One of the best."

"He's lucky to have you."

"We'll see what he has to say about it. He might not want me back."

"Only if he's a fool."

I blushed. "I don't even know your name, and you know all about me."

"I'm Evan," he said, smiling as he extended his hand the short distance between us.

"Abbie." His grip was strong, and I unconsciously winced a little.

"Sorry, I don't know my own strength sometimes. So, I get the feeling there's a story behind this guy you're going after."

"You wouldn't believe me if I told you."

"Ooh, now I'm really interested. It can't be that unusual."

"Trust me—you've never heard anything like this."

He folded his arms across his chest. "You have my attention. Surprise me."

✳ ✳ ✳ ✳ ✳ ✳

"You weren't kidding," he said. "That is some story. Your sister must have called in some serious favors to Santa to get you a man."

"Actually, that's the funniest part," I said, rattling the

ice at the bottom of my cup. "Grace was telling the truth all along. She never wrote the letter; my niece Morgan did. I was accusing her mother for the umpteenth time, and of course, Grace denied it, again. I wasn't really even mad anymore; I just wanted her to own up. Finally, poor Morgan came forward, crying, and admitted that she was the culprit. She said that she was sorry, but she just wanted to do something nice for me. I felt so guilty."

"Oh, man! And I bet your sister went crazy."

"I think she sees it as her responsibility to ensure that I never live it down." It was getting dark in the cabin of the plane now and some of the other passengers were trying to catch a nap before the plane landed. One by one, as I had told Evan my story, nearly all of the tiny overhead beams had blinked out until there were only a few isolated dots of light. "So, what do you think?" I said.

"I think Ben is going to be thrilled to see you again."

"Really?" I realized that my tone was wistful and needy for approval. I still couldn't believe how much I'd come to care for Ben in such a short time. I didn't like to think about how much was riding on his willingness to give me a second chance.

He nodded. "Absolutely. No one goes to that kind of trouble for a girl unless he wants to hold onto her."

"I hope you're right. He'd be completely justified in closing the door in my face."

"Nah, you just weren't ready to make a decision yet. He'll understand."

"So, Evan, who is waiting for you in New York? A girl?" I teased.

"Maybe."

"I thought you were against long-distance relationships."

"This is different."

"Different because it's you?"

"Different because it's my sister."

"You're a good brother to travel such a long way to visit."

"Well, I have to." His proud smile dwarfed his other features. "She just had a baby girl three days ago. I wouldn't be a
very good uncle if I didn't go and introduce myself."

"Congratulations! Is it her first?"

He nodded, pulling a folded up picture from his wallet
and passing it to me. I admired the little bundle of pink with
the wide eyes and the serious expression. "And you don't have
any kids?"

"Naw, haven't met the right girl yet."

"You just wait. You won't be able to say no to your
niece . . . about anything. I have two nieces and a nephew. It's
pathetic how easily I give in."

The pilot's voice came over the speaker, informing us that
we were beginning our descent into New York.

"Almost there now," Evan remarked.

"Don't remind me."

"Don't worry—you'll do fine."

"I'm really glad I met you, Evan."

"Me too. And if for any reason things don't work out with
Ben . . ."

My cheeks colored furiously. "What?"

"I don't know. Maybe you could give me a call?" He scrib-
bled down his phone number on the napkin under his empty
plastic cup, handing it to me bashfully. "Just in case."

✻ ✻ ✻ ✻ ✻ ✻

Back when I started looking for Ben, I went to the book-
store and flipped through travel magazines, searching for his
name on an article. I know I could have just Googled him
online, but for some reason, it was really important to me that
I do this the hard way. It sounds strange, but I felt like taking
a little extra trouble was the least I could do for him. I was
distracted by the glossy pictures of foreign destinations, and
it took a whole afternoon for me to find it, but there it was

finally, big as life: S.B. Carlisle. I traced his name with my finger, feeling my pulse race at the sight of it on the page. It was a confirmation that I had not dreamed the entire episode; Ben was real, his story checked out, and this was proof.

Now that I knew he really existed, I needed a plan. I didn't want to just race in and declare myself. I wanted it to be special, something of the same caliber as what he'd planned for me. I remembered Ben saying that his boss was the only person he'd involved in his scheme to meet me, so I surmised that they must be friends. What was his name . . . something beginning with an L? Larry? Lewis? I went back to the front of the magazine, turning to the page that listed the staff. I scrolled through the credits, my finger stopping on Managing Editor: Leon Maxfield Carlisle. Bingo!

Wait . . . Leon *Carlisle*?

Maybe they were closer than I thought.

I contacted Mr. Carlisle, who turned out to be Ben's dad. I told him who I was and that I needed his help. I was afraid that he might be reluctant to even talk to me, much less help me try to patch things up with his son, but he very kindly assured me that he was willing to assist in any way that he could.

This brings me to the baggage claim . . . and the man waiting, holding a sign that said "Abbie Canfield" in bold, black lettering. I would have recognized him even without the sign; he was an older, more distinguished version of Ben. I approached him with a hesitant smile.

"Miss Canfield?" he said, returning my smile. The similarities between the two men only deepened when he smiled, and something tugged at my heart almost painfully.

"It's Abbie. And you must be Mr. Carlisle."

"I'm very happy to finally meet you. Please, call me Leon. Can I help you with your things?"

I patted the bag slung over my shoulder. "This is it."

"I've got a car waiting outside. Are you ready?"

I hesitated. "Can I ask you something . . . Leon?"

"Of course."

"Is this going to work?"

He shrugged almost apologetically, which I found amusing since I should be the one apologizing. "Your guess is as good as mine. Ben's been a little different since he came back."

"Different?"

He considered his answer. "Withdrawn. He hasn't really talked to me about it much—just little bits and pieces here and there. He came home, said it wasn't meant to be, and plunged right back into work. I don't know what happened while he was with you, but from what I could piece together, he fell hard for someone who didn't return those feelings," he said softly. There was no blame in his words—they were just a statement of fact.

"I did care for Ben, a lot. I just wasn't ready to take the plunge. It wasn't even two weeks. Everything happened so fast."

"You don't have to explain yourself to me. This is between you and my son."

"No, I want you to understand. You've been so good to help me. I never could have done this without you. And you must love Ben a lot to play along."

"For a long time, I thought Ben would never settle down, and it hurt more than I could say when he fell away from the Church." He grinned suddenly. "He's been different in other ways too since he came back. You were good for him, even if the end result wasn't exactly what he was hoping for. I just want to see him happy."

I avoided the positive possibilities of his statement for now. I had to concentrate on one thing at a time, and my immediate focus was on getting Ben to forgive me. I could worry about the rest later. "Which brings me back to my question: you know Ben as well as anyone . . . is this going to work?"

"I've got it outside in the car. Do you want to see it?" he said, extending his arm toward the escalator.

I took a deep breath and followed his lead. "No time like the present."

✳ ✳✳ ✳ ✳ ✳ ✳

"Wow." That was all I could manage to get out. The lights of the city flew past quickly, combining with the whirlwind in my stomach and adding to the illusion that things were spinning out of my control.

"It's quite something to see your name in print, isn't it?"

"It looks so . . . official."

"Yes," he agreed, his eyes twinkling merrily. "Ben was pretty steamed when I told him we were pulling his page this month for a guest columnist. I'm hoping that once he sees this, he might change his mind."

I felt all the color drain from my face. "I hate to have him already angry before I even get started. What if he won't even see me?"

"I'm afraid it's a risk you'll have to take. You're not having second thoughts, are you?" he said quickly. "It's too late to pull it now—the first copies will be on the shelf tomorrow."

"No, I haven't changed my mind. The reason I liked the idea in the first place is because of the permanence of the whole thing. It's just that, if it backfires, it will be so . . . public."

"It's a grand gesture, that's for sure."

"And you're sure he doesn't know anything about it?"

"Positive. No one knew who the guest columnist was but me and the production staff, and they've all been sworn to secrecy."

Suddenly I knew I needed to see Ben now. I couldn't just sit in a hotel room and wait for him to find it tomorrow; it was too excruciating. I had to be there when he saw it. I needed to see the truth in his eyes, to know immediately whether it was enough. I'd spent a long month waiting. I contacted Leon and asked him to help me, but only now did I consider that perhaps I shouldn't have let it go on so long. It seemed like the perfect way to let Ben know the seriousness of my commitment, but not if he'd been suffering in the process.

"Can you take me to Ben's house?" I blurted.

"It's late, Abbie. Don't you want to wait until tomorrow?"

"I really want to see him now."

"After all this time, one more night won't hurt."

"I don't want him to spend one more hour thinking I don't care."

"Are you sure?"

"Positive. Would it be too much trouble for you to drop me off?"

"I'd be happy to, but he won't be there. I'm pretty sure he'll still be at the office."

"But it's almost midnight!"

He shrugged. "He's been working some late hours."

I hesitated. "I don't want to ambush him at work. He has to come home eventually, right?"

"He will, but it might be very late," he warned. "I don't feel right just leaving you on his front step—it's dangerous."

"Don't worry about me; I'll be fine."

We drove in silence until Leon's voice interrupted the quiet. "Can I ask you a question, Abbie? It's kind of personal."

"I guess so."

"What made you change your mind?"

I sighed, attempting to gather my thoughts. I noticed that I was gripping the magazine so tightly that the pages were getting creased. "A long time ago, I made the decision that love was overrated and that I would be happier without the heartache that inevitably seemed to accompany it. When Ben showed up, I was confused and even a little tempted, but I stuck to my convictions. But it took him leaving for me to finally realize that just because I'd been hurt in the past was no reason to send away the best thing that's ever happened to me. I wish now that I hadn't been so stubborn, but I guess some things you just have to learn the hard way."

He looked in my direction, giving me a dazzling smile. "That's good enough for me."

"Let's hope that it's good enough for Ben too," I said, letting out an uneven breath as Leon pulled alongside the curb of an upscale apartment building with several bare trees shivering in front. There were lights in a few of the windows, but most of the tenants appeared to be in bed. I'm sure that during the day it was a very nice place to live, but at night, in an unfamiliar city, it seemed massive and foreboding. I swallowed my trepidation, opening my door to face the freezing weather. I walked around to the driver's side, determined to put on my bravest face.

"Thank you, Leon . . . for everything. I never could have d–d–done it without you," I said, my teeth chattering despite my best efforts. A chill wind began to work its icy magic, pushing through the thin fabric of my coat.

"This is silly. Let me drop you off at your hotel, and I promise I'll bring you back here first thing in the morning," he argued.

"I'm o-k-k-kay. I'll think w-w-warm thoughts. I'm sure B-B-Ben will be back soon."

"It's too cold. I can't have him coming home to find you frozen solid—he'd never forgive me." I hesitated, and Leon's voice went up a tone with concern. "Abbie, your lips are turning blue!"

"I've been told that b-b-b-blue is a good color for m-m-me."

"I thought Ben was exaggerating, but you really are incredibly stubborn, aren't you?"

"Never said I w-w-w-wasn't."

He sighed. "Ben's going to be really angry with me."

"Why?"

"I have a key . . ."

Sixteen

✶ ✳ ✳ ⋅ ❉ ✳ ✳✳ ✦ ✳✳

I sat in a chair at Ben's kitchen table, listening to the steady ticking of the clock on the wall. It seemed like the least intrusive place in the house for me to wait. I already felt like I was trespassing on his life, and I didn't want to make it any worse if I could avoid it. From what I could see of Ben's apartment, it looked very tidy. I was impressed. I could pretty much guarantee that if someone showed up at my house unannounced, it wouldn't be this neat. I was curious about the rest of it, but I forced myself to stay put. I felt like I was snooping just being there. I couldn't help noticing a Book of Mormon sitting on the coffee table when Leon let me in, and I wondered if that was one of the different things about Ben he'd alluded to.

I flipped on a small light in the kitchen, wanting Ben to see me immediately when he came in. I didn't want to scare him, although I knew from experience that when you find someone unexpected in your house, a little fear is inevitable. The soft light made the room seem cozy. I was suddenly exhausted, and the couch in the living room was looking more and more inviting as the clock ticked off the minutes. But even though I was worn out, I knew that I was too wired to sleep. I needed a distraction—something to keep me occupied.

I peeked at the article again while I waited. It was so strange and unnerving, seeing my thoughts printed in a magazine that anyone could pick up and read. When I made the suggestion to Leon, he thought it was a great idea. What better way to make up to Ben than through his own medium? But when I actually sat down to write, it was harder than I thought. How to say what you wanted to say to one person in a public forum eluded me. After endless drafts and some help from Grace, I finally came up with something I was proud of, and as I scanned through the words now, I knew that I had made the right decision.

Travel (and Relationships) for Dummies
By Abbie Canfield

While I enjoy travel, going to exotic places and seeing new things, I do not enjoy packing. In fact, if I didn't have to pack my own things, I would probably travel a lot more. I never get my suitcase out until the last minute, always putting it off as long as possible. There's something so final about trying to anticipate every little thing you might need that always throws me into a panic. Plus, you never know how you're going to feel when you get there. So, even at the eleventh hour, I compulsively over prepare. For example, in your own bedroom, you might feel secure enough for the red two-piece swimsuit you bought when feeling outrageously brave and thin one afternoon, but on the beach, after a heavy dinner, it might be a different story. So I pack three suits, just to be on the safe side: the crazy red one, the dowdy one-piece with a skirt that covers everything, and something in between. I know instinctively that I will go for the something in between option, but you can never be positive until you are in the moment.

My sister gave me a hard time once when we took a trip together. She thinks I'm a terrible packer, but I keep telling her it's all in how you look at it. At least, no one can say I'm not thorough. We got to the room and started unpacking, and she noticed, with great amusement, that I'd packed twelve shirts for a seven-day vacation. Her light teasing turned to howling laughter when she discovered my six pairs of shoes and the eight books I'd stowed away. I informed her haughtily that there's nothing wrong with keeping your options open. After all, who can predict what they will be in the mood to read? That game about being stranded on a desert island for the rest of my life and having to choose five books always makes me come out in a cold sweat.

And then there's the money issue. I'm paranoid about keeping all my money in one place, in case something should happen to that bag. So I tuck it into assorted pockets, wad it up in socks, and fold it into books so that it is evenly distributed. The only problem is that I can't always remember where I hid it. Sometimes I don't find it until I get home and unpack. (And don't even get me started with the unpacking.) Granted, I realize that this is not what might be considered normal behavior, but it seems perfectly logical to me. It's all about being prepared for every eventuality. If there were a merit badge for packing, I would have six.

However, no matter how carefully you check your list when preparing for a trip, inevitably, you forget something. If you're lucky, it's something small like a toothbrush that you can purchase when you reach your destination, or something that you discover you can do without. But sometimes, it's something vital and irreplaceable, and the whole trip is ruined, like the time I forgot the Dramamine when I went boating. Trust me when I say that it's hard enough to get up on water skis when you're not dry-heaving every three minutes.

In case you haven't figured it out yet from the title, this article really isn't a collection of my inane travel ramblings so much as a quirky metaphor on relationships. I know that most of you probably didn't pick up a travel magazine for a discourse on love, but I hope you'll bear with me, as this is a special situation. I don't claim to be an expert on the best beaches or ski resorts, but I do know a thing or two about being prepared . . . or not. It's amazing to me how someone could be so good at one thing, yet completely inept at another. I think it was John Lennon who said that life is what happens to you when you're busy making other plans, and I should know; it happened to me.

I was granted an amazing wish this Christmas. I met someone under rather unorthodox circumstances—someone I never thought I would meet. I told myself in the occasional fantasy that I was pining away for a relationship, that I would give anything if I could only meet a nice guy. But no matter how much I'd convinced myself that I would be thrilled if he magically showed up, the truth was that I simply wasn't ready for it. I wasn't prepared. I hesitated, and it cost me something really important.

I heard a key turn in the lock and froze momentarily. This was it, and I wasn't ready. Instead of fawning over the article, I should have been rehearsing what to say. I waited helplessly for the door to open with absolutely no idea of what to do next. As Ben's familiar face appeared, I had the overwhelming impression that everything was going to be all right. He paused in the doorway, staring at me like I was a ghost—seeing me, yet not seeing me.

"Hey," I said finally, my voice a full range higher than it should have been.

"Hey, yourself." He never took his eyes off me the whole time he was locking the door and hanging his coat on the rack. He didn't look angry, but he didn't exactly look pleased to see me either. Pretty much he just looked shocked. He moved a bit nearer, still keeping plenty of distance between us. As he crept closer, his eyes darted around the room, surveying it cautiously.

"I guess you know how I felt now, finding you under my Christmas tree," I said, a feeble attempt at humor.

"Not exactly. You invited me in with that letter, remember?"

I winced, kicking myself mentally for not following Leon's advice and coming back tomorrow. "I'm sorry, I really should have called, but a surprise seemed like a good idea at the time."

"You've succeeded beyond your wildest dreams." Some of the color was starting to flood back into his face. He walked across the room until he was just feet away from me, at the other end of the small table. Either he'd somehow gotten even better looking in a month, or my memories didn't do him justice. Other than the fact that his face looked drawn and tired, it was just about the most welcome sight I'd ever beheld. A frown creased his forehead, and his eyes still roamed across the room. It was starting to make me nervous.

"What are you looking for?" I asked, unable to take it anymore.

"Broken glass."

I gaped at him. "You think I broke into your apartment?"

"Well, you had to get in somehow, and I don't have a chimney."

"You live on the eleventh floor," I said incredulously. "I'd have had to scale the building before breaking a window was even an option."

"Right. You'll have to excuse me, but my brain is a little fuzzy. I haven't been sleeping very well lately."

I stood up tentatively. "Maybe I should go—you look tired."

"You're here, so you might as well stay awhile. What's that in your hand?"

"In-flight magazine," I said, tucking it into my duffel bag. After the reception I'd gotten so far, there was no way I was ready to go down that road just yet. The voice in my head had a new mantra. Over and over, it repeated, *Bad idea, bad idea, bad idea . . .* and I found myself questioning why I ever thought this would work. I twisted my hands together nervously, finally forcing myself to look into Ben's face again. I saw a bare hint of a smile, and it made me bold all at once. "So, I notice you didn't return the favor."

"What favor?"

"I believe I left my door unlocked for you on a regular basis."

"Are you crazy? You can't leave your house unlocked in New York! If you do, you come home to find everything you own cleaned out. In fact, sometimes they even take the door."

"I guess that's fair." My heart was pounding so hard in my chest that I could hardly hear my own voice over the racket. I knew that if I waited much longer, I would never be able to say what I came to say. I could quite easily see myself going home without ever saying a word. It would be simpler than putting myself out there, only to be shot down. "What have you been up to?" I said lamely, my eyes fixed on the table as I tried to say something to break the uncomfortable silence and keep the conversation moving forward.

"I actually spent some time in the hospital. They wanted to do some tests on my heart."

My head snapped up. "What's wrong with your heart?"

He shrugged. "I thought it was broken, but the doctors told me they couldn't find anything wrong with it."

I groaned. "That isn't funny. You shouldn't scare me like that. I was really worried."

"I'm sorry, but it was too perfect. I might never get a chance to use that line again. How about you—what have you been doing?"

"Making a lot of cupcakes."

"Is that significant?"

"Every since I was a girl, when I get sad, I make cupcakes," I admitted.

"I like cupcakes."

I snorted. "Not after eating them every day for a month you wouldn't. The customers were beginning to think I'd lost my mind." I was starting to feel slightly more at ease; this seemed like a conversation we might have had before, when everything was okay. I don't know how much time passed while I considered how to proceed, but Ben finally interrupted my scattered thoughts.

"Not that I'm unhappy to see you, but what are you doing here, Abbie?" He said it gently, in a way that was not unkind, but I could tell that he was baffled by this turn of events. I felt tears welling up in my eyes, but I knew that I couldn't start crying now. I squeezed my eyes shut, forcing back the flood. I needed to be calm and collected in order to plead my case.

"Do you always work so late?" I asked.

"Not always. I've been pretty busy lately."

My heart was reaching flying speed. It was now or never.

"Really?" I said, trying to keep the insane tension from my voice. "I would have thought you'd be bored, since they gave your column to someone else this month."

There. I'd done it. It would all come out now. Ball in his court.

"How would you know about that?" he said slowly.

"Leon told me."

"How do you know Leon?" he demanded.

I hurried on while he tried to process everything. "Do you really call your dad Leon?"

"Yes, at work." He blinked, putting together yet another piece of the puzzle. "How do you know Leon is my dad?"

I smiled. The deeper I got, the easier it was. "I remembered you mentioning that your editor, Leon, was the only person you told about me, so I figured you must be pretty close. I tracked him down because I was hoping that he would be willing to help me with a little project I had in mind."

"What kind of project?"

I felt the fear creeping in again, but only for a second. There was a miraculous warmth spreading through my chest, pushing away all my doubts and questions. I was certain now that I'd done the right thing. Whether Ben still wanted me or not, I knew in that moment that I would not have to look forward to a future of regret, always wondering what might have been if I had tried. My conscience would be clear.

I retrieved the magazine from where I'd hidden it in the depths of my bag, handing it across to Ben with shaking hands.

"This is my magazine," he said uncertainly.

"Not this month." There was a small degree of smugness that I was unable to swallow, and it leaked out in my triumphant presentation.

He stared at the cover, still not managing to make the connection. I flipped to the page impatiently, so that he could be in no doubt of my intentions. He looked at the title and byline, startling me with an unexpected laugh. There was a look of something very like admiration on his face, and he was wide awake now. "Would you read it to me?" he asked hesitantly.

I took it from him and began to read it, my voice shaky with a strange combination of excitement and dread. He snickered at my travel issues, and I managed to get to the point where I'd abruptly stopped reading before, when Ben arrived. My voice suddenly became thick with overwhelming emotion. I tried to regain control of the situation, wanting to hang on long enough to do this right. As I struggled, I felt Ben's hand resting on my shoulder.

"May I?" he offered.

I surrendered it to him gratefully, listening while he read the rest of it to me.

Now, a few words for you, my Christmas present. You said that maybe I'd never really been in love before, and you were probably right. I think that I finally understand what love is and, more importantly, what it isn't. Love is not the thousand sticky sweet sentiments of greeting cards and romantic movies. Love is something stronger, and sometimes less attractive. Love is having something you can count on in this world where you can depend on nothing, and learning that it's okay to let someone else shovel the driveway for a change. And love is patiently waiting while someone you care about catches up. In short, love is what you were trying to show me, but I was too afraid to listen. Like the Dramamine, I've been forced to discover the hard way that you're one of the important things, one of the things I can't do without.

As I write this, the snow is still falling softly in my little corner of the world. It looks as if Santa might drop by any minute in his sleigh with his eight tiny reindeer. But Christmas has passed this year, and I let it go by without taking advantage of the miraculous opportunity I was offered. It seems a bit selfish to be requesting another chance, but I just wanted you to know that if you're still interested, all I want for Christmas is you . . . for real, this time. I can't promise anything, but I'm willing to give it a try.

Are you?

Ben shook his head in disbelief, his own eyes bright now. "I can't believe you were so brave. I should have known you had it in you, after the sledding episode."

"I'm not brave. I was terrified—just like I am now."

"Why are you terrified?" he asked, his voice soft and mystified.

"Because I don't know what you're thinking. I've put myself in this precarious position, and you have all the control . . . which is not unlike the sledding, now that I think about it."

"I don't know what you're so worried about. I told you what I wanted already."

"But that was a long time ago."

"A month isn't such a long time."

"It sure seemed like a long time."

He grinned. "Yeah, it did."

Ben paused then, and I didn't know if he was weighing his options or just dragging out the suspense. I realized that I was holding my breath. I tried to let it out a little at a time, so that it wasn't so obvious how very much I depended on his next words.

"When I was a little boy, my older brother—"

"You have an older brother?" I interrupted, wondering at this abrupt change in topic.

"Matt. He wanted to play baseball, more than anything. But he was kind of puny, and he wasn't very good. So, one summer he spent hours every day developing his pitching arm. He threw the ball against the side of the house over and over, until I thought my mother was going to have a nervous breakdown. He just kept lobbing that ball at the wall until I was sure his arm would fall off. He played catch with my dad. He built up his muscles. He did everything he could to ensure that he would make the team at school, because that was his dream."

"I suppose you're going to tell me that Matt is a professional baseball player now or something."

"No, he's a lawyer. He never even made the high school team because he was terrible. I made the team though, and I didn't even like baseball that much. It took a long time for him to forgive me."

"O-kaaay. So, why did you tell me that story, exactly, besides to brag that you were good at sports?"

"The story wasn't about sports; it was about persistence. The point is that even though Matt wasn't very good, he kept trying. He knew what he wanted, and he went for it."

" . . . and failed miserably," I concluded.

"Abbie, it means that as long as you're willing to try, I'll be here. But I can't do this again if you're going to sit on the fence. I understand that there's a chance this might not work out, but I need to know that it will be because we discover that we're incompatible or you make terrible meatloaf, not because you're afraid. Can you do that?"

"Weren't you listening when I read the article?" I said in a mock-scolding tone.

He walked to where I was sitting, offering me his hand. I tentatively slipped my fingers into his palm, and his fingers curled around mine. He pulled me out of the chair and into his arms, and I knew that even with all the difficulty I had under-taken to get to this point, it was worth it if I got to spend even another minute wrapped in these arms that knew me.

"Just checking," he said, whispering the words into my neck. He moved his head so that he could see my face, and his eyes shone with a mischievous light. "I've missed your lips. My lips barely had a chance to get acquainted with them."

"It all seems so strange now—almost like I dreamed that time we spent together."

"Don't you hate that? When you wake up before the dream ends and you never find out what happens?"

"Shall I tell you what happens?"

"I'm all ears."

"Once upon a time, there was an independent but lonely girl who wrote a letter, asking for the one unspoken thing that she never imagined was possible. A lonely but very wise man took her challenge. He called her bluff, and she retreated. But there was something that the girl didn't realize until after he was gone."

To Ben's credit, he played along. "What?"

"In the short time he knew her, he managed to do what no other guy ever had."

"Successfully break into her house on more than one occasion?"

"No. Guess again."

"Force her into sledding with disastrous results?"

"No, silly. He stole her heart."

"And they lived happily . . . ever . . . after?" Ben asked, leaning in and planting three short but soft kisses on my lips in rapid succession.

"There's only one way to find out."